DEDICATION

This autobiographical fiction novel is dedicated to Spike. Although he has been in doggie heaven for decades, I cherish his memory daily.

Spike

by

Chip Bock

This novel is based on an actual journey, but the story has
been embellished and fictionalized.

ISBN-13: 978-0-9982972-2-4

ACKNOWLEDGMENTS

Foremost, I want to thank my wife Audrey for her companionship during the writing of this novel.
I want to thank Tiffany Morse, my very competent and knowledgeable editor, who turned my awful grammar and sentence structure into a professional work.
I also want to thank Kara Noble McCoy for her wonderful book cover design.
Finally, I want to thank my childhood friend Jeff Shear. Jeff is a professional writer who mentored me on the business of writing.

CONTENTS

Prologue

Spike was a springer spaniel, about three years old, and was a roommate to Sebastian, a recent college graduate in his mid-twenties. They lived in the Pocono Mountains, near many of the popular honeymoon resorts that are situated throughout the northeastern Pennsylvania mountains. The Appalachian trail runs through this part of the country. Not long ago Sebastian had graduated with his bachelor's degree and was feeling unfulfilled. He didn't want a career yet and had a lot of unanswered questions about life.

One day, a friend of his from the nearby college said he was going out West as part of an expedition to study biological specimens, fauna, and topographic phenomena. Sebastian, who had neither a car nor much cash, thought maybe he could catch a ride with the caravan.

When he arrived the morning of departure, the caravan was lined up with many cars. He asked the expedition leader, but nobody had room for him and Spike. The caravan left without them. Sebastian sighed, gave Spike a pat, and decided that he and Spike would go West anyway, even without a car. He had hitchhiked many times before, just not on such a long trip. This began their quest for adventure and, hopefully, some enlightenment along the way.

Chapter 1

The journey began on a warm, spring day. Sebastian, a tall lanky youth in his twenties, stood on the side of the road, his thumb stuck out to passing cars, while his dog, Spike, watched. The two were embarking on a trip with no specific destination, just hoping to seek out new places and adventures. Sebastian was searching and thought that maybe life would gain more meaning and he would gain a greater understanding of God and the universe. As for Spike, he was just happy to be with Sebastian.

Spike, a full-breed English springer spaniel, had long curly ears that drooped in his water bowl when he drank. His liver-and-white color graced his 55 pounds very nicely. He had a white streak that ran down the center of his snoot, with white also covering his paws. His tail had been snipped off early in life, probably in his first weeks alive. When it wagged, it wiggled his whole back end. He was very possessive of Sebastian; they were best pals. Sebastian had raised him since he was a seven-week-old puppy. Spike was now about three years old and had never been on a leash. Living in the mountains, he was able to roam free without the hindrance of leash laws. When in urban areas, he would stay near Sebastian when they walked and wait outside if ever Sebastian had to go into a building.

Waiting patiently, the two were quite a pair. Sebastian, with his shoulder-length curly hair, wore jeans, work boots, a t-shirt, and backpack. Spike wore his usual brown-and-white outfit. After watching cars, trucks, and motorcycles blow past them long enough for Sebastian's arm to get tired, a blue Chevy Impala pulled over. A couple in their early thirties greeted them with smiles.

Sebastian believed in a hitchhiker's code of ethics. Since these people were nice and hospitable enough to give him a ride, it was his duty to make the driver and passengers feel at ease. Sebastian thought it would be downright rude to make someone feel uncomfortable in their own vehicle. Spike, his tail wagging, broke the ice.

"Where are you heading?" the driver asked Sebastian, while his wife petted Spike.

"We are heading west, toward California," answered Sebastian.

"And what is your purpose out West?" asked the driver, with no apparent cynicism in his voice.

"No particular purpose, sir. Only to have some new experiences, see the country, and maybe find some meaning in life along the way," replied Sebastian.

"I don't mean any disrespect to you, but I find it very unusual to be hitchhiking with a dog and expect to find the meaning of life."

"You may be absolutely right. I may not find any meaning at all, yet something inside of me says that I've got to try anyway," said Sebastian.

The conversation continued off and on throughout the trip. Spike laid across the back seat with his face in Sebastian's lap. By doing so, if he fell asleep, he would awake if Sebastian got up. He didn't want his buddy out of his sight.

The couple were on their way to western Pennsylvania to visit relatives. The sister of the driver was getting married. The conversation focused on weddings and relationships between relatives. Sebastian was eager to listen to the driver's attitude toward the wedding, so he was quite attentive, which kept the driver talking. He was upset because he wasn't chosen to be in the wedding party. Sebastian tried to assure him that it was no personal affront, just that the groom had many brothers and good friends himself. This soothed the driver and got him smiling again. They finally reached the last Pittsburgh exit, and they let Sebastian and Spike out.

There stood the two by the side of the road, a scenario that would be repeated time and again throughout their journey. The next vehicle took them on a short ride into Ohio. By then, the sun was beginning to set. The pair sought out a hidden spot away from the roadside, laid out a sleeping bag, and went to sleep. Spike laid his snoot across Sebastian's torso, carefully guarding his lifelong pal and caretaker. Although appearing to sleep, any sound opened his eyes, increasing his awareness. While Sebastian slept, Spike was in the protective mode and nothing would get past his watch.

The morning sun came early, lifting their lids with each ascent in the dawn sky. Sebastian dug in his backpack for breakfast—a couple handfuls of granola for him, and for Spike, his usual dog food. Sebastian never made Spike carry a backpack filled with his own food and supplies like many hikers who walk the Appalachian trail. He didn't like to think of his dog as a mule, feeling it might kill his spirit. With bellies satisfied, the pair made their way back to the road.

It was a glorious morning, fresh and crisp. The pair stood patiently until a pickup truck pulled over. The driver leaned over and said get in. Sebastian put Spike in the bed and then got in the front seat.

"How far are you going?" the driver asked.

Sebastian suddenly turned to look more closely. He recognized that voice.

"Charlie? Is that you?"

A big smile covered the driver's face; he couldn't believe it was Sebastian. The two had been best buddies in the army while stationed overseas. Both had been discharged honorably a few years earlier. A lot of veterans say they will get together, but time and distance prevent a lot of those friendships from continuing.

They couldn't believe their reunion was taking place at 6 a.m. on the Ohio interstate. Charlie, who had a stable home life with a wife and child, was quite shocked at Sebastian's lifestyle, and maybe a little envious of the freedom. The time went quickly as they began telling old stories.

Charlie said, "Remember the time when we went on our motorcycles up to El Valle, that resort up by the Costa Rican border? The guy was playing a Spanish guitar as the Pacific Ocean waves broke below, and we ate a nice lobster meal for just a couple dollars?"

"The drinks were good and the smell of hemp was in the air," Sebastian added.

They both laughed. Their MOS (Military Occupational Specialty) had been serving in the Military Police, specifically the United States Southern Command Military Prison.

Sebastian said, "How about the time those prisoners were in the cell armed with lead pipes and other tools, and we were ordered to get them out? That was pretty wild."

Sebastian, who had never trained as an MP but rather as a company clerk, was often given a .45 pistol and told to take prisoners to appointments.

"You know," he said, "I'd take those guys to see their dentist or lawyer or someone, and I would think what am I going to do if a prisoner runs away?"

Charlie glanced at him. "What would you have done?"

Sebastian shook his head. "I would have shot in the air and just said I missed."

Charlie nodded. "Sounds like something you'd do."

"Most of those guys were in for nonviolent offenses anyway."

They chattered the whole hour. Neither had been in touch with any other soldiers from their unit. However, Sebastian had plans to look up a mutual friend when he arrived in Los Angeles. Charlie gave Sebastian a message to take with him.

Suddenly, Charlie's exit arrived. He pulled to the side, they shook hands, smiled, and that was the last time the two would ever speak to each other.

Not long did Sebastian and Spike wait before a full-size sedan stopped. A gentleman with a white button-down short-sleeved shirt brought the passenger-side power window down and said, "Hop in."

Sebastian put Spike in the back seat, and he got in the front.

Sebastian knew that people stopped for hitchhikers for many reasons. Some may have hitchhiked in the past themselves, or they may just have a spiritual morality to help out their fellow man. Some lived very boring lives and lived vicariously through the adventures of less stable individuals. However, Sebastian did realize there were also unscrupulous scoundrels lurking along the highways, waiting for an opportunity to perform evil, selfish acts. He just hoped that their paths didn't cross. If they did, he would have to deal with it as it came. Sebastian knew that evil can find its way even into one's own living room or bedroom, but he wasn't going to let fear dictate his life's activities.

"You been traveling long?" said the gentleman.

"No, actually we are just beginning our trip," replied Sebastian.

"What's the purpose of your travel?" asked the driver.

"No particular purpose. Just seeking some meaningful experiences."

"If you want some meaningful experiences, why don't you go to church? In fact, why don't you come to my church. Tomorrow is Sunday. You can join us in celebration of our Lord and Savior, Jesus Christ. We have a nice backyard—you can pitch a tent, spend the night at our house, and get saved tomorrow. I'm Walter, by the way."

Sebastian thought a moment and then said to the gentleman, "We accept your hospitable invitation."

They arrived at the house after a two-hour ride. It was a small house in a small town in rural Indiana. The house had a white picket fence encircling it and about two acres of cut green grass. Sebastian and Spike went to the back and pitched a small green backpacking tent.

Sebastian was invited in for dinner. He told Spike to stay by the tent, and the spaniel obeyed. Once inside, Sebastian was offered use of their guest bathroom to shower. As he dried off, he looked in the mirror at his wet, curly hair and thick, dark beard. He thought about what a strange situation this was. These seemed to be nice God-loving people who had opened up their house and their privacy to a ragged looking hitchhiker and his dog.

Sebastian then went to the dining room for a sit-down dinner. There on the table was a Thanksgiving-type dinner. Turkey with stuffing, mashed potatoes, gravy, green beans, cranberries, candied yams, homemade biscuits and butter. Sebastian had not told the man that he was a vegetarian. He just filled his plate with everything but the turkey, somehow hoping they wouldn't notice. Before they ate, they held hands and recited a prayer thanking God for the food on the table.

"Sebastian, this is my wife Lillian, the best darn cook in Lorber County."

The woman blushed and lowered her eyes upon hearing the compliment.

"Very nice to meet you, ma'am, and thank you very much for the hospitality. This is the best meal I've had in a couple years."

The woman's eyes brightened up the room after hearing that remark. She was a plain but sweet-looking woman in her mid-forties. She wore an ankle-length dress and a cross on a necklace. Her shoulder-length brown hair was parted down the middle and tucked behind her ears exposing a freckled face with a few wrinkles around the eyes.

It was quiet while they ate, but in between bites, Walter talked about their congregation a lot, often with food still inside his cheeks. Walter, a big man of about six feet and 235 pounds, had a large gut that hung over his belt. He probably never exercised and ate these meals every week. His thinning blonde hair, shaved above the ears, exposed a conservative lifestyle. However, Sebastian always made a point of trying not to judge people, especially based on their looks. People can be very different from their outer shell. In fact, Sebastian was a good example of that premise. When they finished off the last bite of apple pie and ice cream, Sebastian thanked them and said good night. Walter said that they would attend nine o'clock services. Sebastian agreed.

"Good morning," said Sebastian as he joined the couple for breakfast before church.

They enjoyed a hearty spread of scrambled eggs, sausage, hash brown potatoes, and homemade biscuits. He thanked them but only had some orange juice and toast. Before they left for church, Sebastian fed Spike, gave him fresh water, and told him to stay by the tent. Spike listened and laid down. He didn't like it when Sebastian left, but he obeyed the order.

When the door opened to the church, the pews were almost filled already. All eyes turned to look at this strange-looking character. Sebastian felt like a freak in a carnival side show, but he knew this was part of the exploration process, so what the hell! The men all wore slacks, button-down shirts and ties. Some even wore jackets. He greeted them with his old, faded blue jeans, a jean jacket, a red t-shirt, and a red bandanna tied around his neck. His curly locks hung over his collar.

They sat down in the tenth row just before the service started. After the initial greeting and prayer, the minister personally greeted Sebastian as a guest in their church. Sebastian smiled and noted acknowledgment of the gesture. There were a lot of Hallelujahs, hand-holding, preaching of the Word, and some singing. Sebastian tried to fit in, but inside he knew that he might as well have been an interplanetary alien. All the little kids looked down the rows and giggled to each other. Everyone was amiable, though, and wished him well as he left the church.

On the drive home, Sebastian told Walter and Lillian that he and Spike would be on their way. Walter nodded and said that he would drive them back to the highway.

On arrival at the house, Spike was wiggling his whole body at the joy of his returning master. Sebastian petted Spike and took the tent down, gathered his backpack and bowls. He thanked his hosts with a handshake and a hug and got into the car. This was a good day, he thought. The couple lived the true Christian spirit; they were the backbone of American civilization. These no-frills, hard-working people were the glue that kept many communities together.

Chapter 2

Overcast and warm, the weather looked a little threatening. Sebastian knew that he was in tornado country. Indiana was flat, and the topography provoked wind spouts this time of year. He didn't want to be caught on the open highway if a spout began to develop. It wasn't long before a blue Chevrolet van stopped. The driver was a young man in his late twenties with a ponytail. Beside him was an attractive girl with long, straight, blonde hair. She wore a white tank top and cut-off blue jeans. They called her Sheila. The driver told Sebastian to get in and flipped him the peace sign. As Sebastian got in, he noticed that the van reeked of something similar to burnt rope. Sebastian had smelled that before and knew that it wasn't really rope.

"Hey, dude, how you doing?" said another young man as he sucked on a big rolled-up cigarette. As he put out his hand to give the cigarette to Sebastian, he said, "This bud's for you."

Sebastian, wanting to keep his wits about him but not wanting to appear threatening, said, "Man, sorry, but we're on a totally spiritual quest this summer."

"That's cool. I totally respect you for it. Actually, I've been thinking about making the switch myself."

Sebastian was quite relieved that his negative response wasn't met with hostility. He nodded to the fourth person in the van, another girl in her early twenties with curly brunette hair, a tie-dyed sundress, and sandals. She was giving Spike wheat crackers. He was sitting there on the floor of the van, lifting his paw up, looking with those sad eyes; he had her where he wanted her. The van was dark, curtains covered many of the windows, and Jimi Hendrix was playing "All Along the Watchtower" on the 8-track.

"How far are you going?" asked the driver.

"Heading west," replied Sebastian.

"Good. You can hang with us. We're going to Colorado."

Sebastian relaxed. He was tired and just wanted to rest. These people seemed really nice, and Spike had a good friend already—at least as long as the cracker box was full. Sebastian drifted off to sleep, as did Spike, who was sprawled out at his feet.

They were both awakened by the sound of the siren of an Illinois state police officer. Sebastian, dazed and confused by the siren, looked around the van. He didn't know these people's personal histories, but he realized that he would be included in their group if laws had been broken.

The officer cautiously approached the driver's side of the van and said, "Let me have your driver's license and registration, please."

The pony-tailed driver, Rich, replied, "No problem, officer. Can you tell me why I'm being pulled over?" He smiled a big shit-eating grin, his eyes glossy.

"I'm stopping you because your rear taillight is busted." He then went back to his police car to radio in the license and check on the driver's record.

The officer quickly came back to the van and said, "Where are you going?" He shined a light into the vehicle, looking around at all the passengers.

"We're all heading to Colorado. We heard it's an awesome place to visit," replied Rachel, the one who was feeding Spike crackers.

"A bunch of hippies, are you?" the officer asked with a disapproving look on his face.

"Well, that depends on your definition of a hippy," answered Rich.

"Don't give me any of your lip or smart aleck answers or I'll have you before the local constable in the morning."

Sebastian didn't like the way this meeting was going. Many scenarios of how this might end began to flash through his mind.

The officer slowly walked around the van looking in the windows. Then he said, "Will all of you please come outside? I want to have a look around."

One by one, they all quietly stepped out of the van. As the officer peeked into the back of the van, he felt something wet on his face. He pulled back very quickly, and then, after shining his light, he realized that it was Spike's tongue that had slurped his face.

He turned and asked, "Who's springer spaniel is this?"

Sebastian immediately saw four fingers pointing in his direction.

The officer's demeanor quickly began to change, and, believe it or not, a smile came across his face. He replied, "I raise springer spaniels as a side profession, and this dog has as nice markings as ninety percent of this breed. Do you ever use him as a stud?"

Sebastian said no, thinking about all the ramifications of being a stud. Certainly nobody had ever asked him to do that. The officer talked to Sebastian for a good fifteen minutes about Spike, petting the dog the whole time.

Finally, he said to Rich, "I'm giving you a warning about your light."

He then shook hands with Sebastian and gave him a business card that read "Ringers Springers, a spaniel for Sport and Family, owned by Sgt. Phillip Ringer" before driving away.

They all breathed sighs of relief and gave Spike an extra pet. Sebastian felt comfort in the fact that he and Spike had just saved their asses, and not just from a ticket. He suspected that they probably had some illegal substances hidden in the van, which the officer could not have overlooked had he found them. Sebastian began to think about making alternative arrangements the next day.

That night during the ride across Illinois, Sebastian had quite a few in-depth conversations with the group. They were old, school buddies who had grown up in Atlantic City and gone to Atlantic City High School together. Rich had trained in plumbing and heating after graduation and now apprenticed for his uncle.

Rachel, his girlfriend, worked as a waitress at a bar in Somers Point, N.J., called the Fantasy Queen. Sebastian asked her about the meaning of the name.

She said, "We have girls dancing while wearing very little, which gives many men an open-ended fantasy."

Sebastian asked, "Do they also satisfy men's fantasies there?"

"No. At least not on the premises. We would be shut down in a minute. Now, what they do in the parking lot or at home is their own business."

Then there was Mel. He owned a submarine shop a block off the boardwalk in Atlantic City. His uncle, who had recently been laid off from a job with Union Carbide, was running the store for him. The last of the group, Jimmy, was a short guy with a receding hairline. He worked as a salad man at the Deauville Hotel dining room. He had recently given his leave of absence to go on this trip.

Sebastian had a good rapport with the group. They were curious about his adventures and his background. They laughed, drank a little Mateus Rosé wine together, and told funny stories.

"Once, in high school," Sebastian told Rachel, "I was visiting Atlantic City. This was in the days when thousands of teenagers would crowd the beach on Memorial Day, July 4th, and Labor Day."

"Did your parents let you go alone?" asked Rachel.

"Later, as a senior, but as a freshman, on this trip, my older brother took me and I stayed at a motel with two of his friends," he said. "One day, I was minding my own business, walking on the boardwalk, and I looked up at the Claridge Hotel. Every window had some guy's bare ass pressed against it. The kids on the beach, thousands of them, were in an uproar. I heard sirens. Then I saw hundreds of kids running out of the Claridge hotel toward me, and I knew the police were probably chasing them. So I turned around and started running, too."

"Oh! Why did you start running?"

"I didn't want to be mistaken as part of the group."

"Right." Rachel nodded.

"I ran off the boardwalk—I'm not sure why!—and all these kids followed me. I took another turn, and they followed me again. 'What's going on?' I thought. 'They must think I'm their leader or something.' I ducked in an alley and watched as many of those kids who passed me were soon being loaded into police paddy wagons."

Rachel let out a high-pitched giggle. "Oh, that's too much!"

The group took turns driving through the night while Sebastian and Spike slept soundly. They awoke at the break of dawn. Sebastian saw signs for Kansas City, thirty miles ahead. He told them to let him off in Topeka, which was just a few hours away down Route 70. Luckily, the rest of the trip with the Atlantic City group was uneventful and friendly. Sebastian and Spike exited the van at the second Topeka exit, said their goodbyes, and the van sped off with the taillight still broken.

Chapter 3

The sky was clear, temperature in the upper 70s, and it was only 9 a.m. Sebastian and Spike walked off the interstate and found an open supermarket. Sebastian wanted to restock a few supplies. He went inside while Spike waited outside, leashless. Sebastian didn't like leashes. He wouldn't want one on himself, so why put one on Spike? Spike stayed with him, as any good pal would. He kept a leash in the backpack, just in case it was necessary. He filled up his canteen with water, bought an apple and banana, some granola, dog biscuits, and they were ready to go.

At the entrance of the interstate, they waited a couple hours before a light blue Plymouth station wagon stopped. A young woman in her early thirties leaned over to roll down the window. She had shoulder-length brunette hair, parted down the middle. She had on blue jean cut-offs, sandals, and a button-down light blue blouse with no sleeves. An antique black and white cameo necklace hung from her neck, snuggled by her cleavage. She asked Sebastian where they were heading, and he told her out West.

"Hop in," she said.

Spike jumped into the back of the wagon, next to Sebastian's backpack and a beat up red Samsonite suitcase. Then Sebastian slid into the front passenger seat. He and the woman exchanged pleasantries quickly, Sebastian trying to make her feel free of fear immediately. She introduced herself as Wendy.

"What are you doing hitchhiking out west with a dog?" Wendy asked.

"Spike and I are just hanging out and maybe looking for a bit of God along the way," replied Sebastian.

"I'm visiting a Buddhist retreat for a week somewhere near the foothills of Pike's Peak, Colorado. You can come along for the ride. It's a long trip across Kansas and half of Colorado. I could use the company. By the way, do you have a driver's license?"

"Yes. In fact, I'm a pretty good driver, in case you should need my help."

After a moment of silence, Wendy said, "I've been involved with the teachings of Buddha for the last couple of years. I used to be an Episcopalian, but I found that unrewarding. I was searching for some spiritual meaning when I heard a Zen Buddhist monk speak at a local community college. It just grabbed me, and I haven't let go since."

"It must be the right path for you to follow at this time. You should always follow your inner feelings," said Sebastian.

During their conversations, whenever Wendy made a point, she would press on Sebastian's thigh or upper arm. Sebastian didn't mind it at all. In fact, he quite cherished the human warmth.

"What do you do for a living?" asked Sebastian.

"I help my parents with the family business, an asphalt paving company. We have contracts with the state and other commercial corporations. I usually handle the bookkeeping and office work. However, my passion lies elsewhere."

His curiosity sparked, Sebastian asked, "What exactly is that passion?" He leaned toward her with interest.

"I've been going to school at night to be a massage therapist. I like the hands-on approach to life. Have you ever had a massage?" she inquired.

"Never had a professional massage. I've never had much extra money for those kinds of luxuries," replied Sebastian.

Wendy began to discuss all the positive attributes of massage and the various schools, such as Shiatsu, Swedish, and deep tissue. Sebastian was curious and pressed against parts of her body asking if this is how they do it. His touch gave her goose bumps.

They took turns driving, switching every couple of hours. The sky started to get dim as the sun began to set behind the mountains in the far distance. Wendy suggested they stop and rest. Sebastian, traveling with very little money, said he had a tent and sleeping bag.

Wendy said, "Don't worry about it. I've got money. We'll get a roadside motel room."

Sebastian agreed, never one to be disagreeable. Spike was anxious to get out of the car and retrieve the rubber ball that Sebastian kept in his pack.

They saw a sign for Prairie Dog Motel and pulled in. As soon as the car stopped, Spike leaped out with the ball, dropped it, and then barked for Sebastian to throw it. Sebastian obliged, and Spike retrieved it. This repeated many times.

They checked into unit 8. As the door flung open, they scanned the room and saw a clean but small room with seasoned oak panel walls and a small bedside table with matching lights on either side of the queen bed which was covered with a homemade quilt. To the right and back of the bed was a bathroom, and a small desk stood on the far right with a New Testament Bible. Just to the right of the door was a black-and-white 18-inch TV with antenna.

Sebastian offered to let Wendy clean up first. She appreciated the gentlemanly courtesy. While she showered, he read a novel that he carried in his backpack. She came out, white towels wrapped around both her body and hair, revealing long thin legs and firm voluptuous breasts.

Sebastian then quickly showered. He washed his long, curly hair and shook it dry. As he came out of the bathroom, Wendy lifted up the sheets, signaling him to slip under the sheets with her. Never one to hurt someone's feelings, Sebastian did as she indicated.

Wendy said, "I'm going to give you your first professional massage."

Sebastian's eyes sparkled.

"Let's start with your back."

Sebastian turned over, arms outstretched. Wendy straddled his upper thighs and pressed her palms firmly over his scapulas and shoulder joints. Her fingers began to knead his deep muscles.

"You're tense," she said, as she continued to work.

Sebastian began to relax and the tenseness disappeared. As Wendy leaned forward and massaged his shoulders, Sebastian could feel her breasts caressing his back. Sebastian thought, There really is a God, and He is shining His light on me. The massage proceeded, progressing to intimacy, and the two drifted off to sleep together. Spike stayed right at Sebastian's bedside.

The morning sun intruded on their sleep as it shone through the slit between the flowered curtains.

Wendy rolled over, kissed Sebastian on the cheek, and whispered, "Good morning."

He awakened and greeted her with a warm smile. One thing led to another, and they were intimate one more time before they packed up and checked out.

As they were packing the car, Wendy felt her neck and stood motionless. Sebastian noticed that she looked pale and inquired if she was all right.

Wendy said, "My cameo necklace is missing. It was given to me by my great-grandmother before she died."

In a frantic state, Wendy raced around the room and property looking, but to no avail. She was petrified at the thought of it disappearing. Sebastian grabbed her shaking hand, and together they both looked again, but still no cameo. Just then, Spike came running up, tail wagging, with a piece of jewelry in his mouth. Wendy was ecstatic, hugging and kissing the liver-and-white springer spaniel. Spike had earned a few extra biscuits.

They all got back in the wagon, Wendy feeling great relief knowing that her family heirloom was intact and with her. And so a new day began.

Chapter 4

With Wendy in the passenger's seat, Sebastian drove toward the wall of the Rocky Mountain landscape. It jettisoned to the sky from the flat Colorado plains.

"Awesome," Wendy whispered.

Sebastian nodded. "Incredible."

They saw a sign for Route 24, a smaller road that led to the Colorado Springs area.

"Would you like to come with me to the Buddhist retreat?" asked Wendy.

"I'm not a Buddhist," said Sebastian, "but do they allow dogs in their camp?"

Wendy shrugged. "We can try. If not, I'll take you to a nearby interstate or town."

"That sounds fair to me. This might be an enlightening adventure. Besides that," he added, "a little more time with you is worth the detour."

Wendy hugged him and kissed him on the cheek.

The Plymouth wagon veered off Route 70 and headed west on Route 24 toward Colorado Springs. They drove through town, picking up Route 25 North. They could feel the car straining from the long climb up the mountains. The temperature and oil gauges had opposing effects. The temperature kept rising, and the oil level kept declining. They stopped at an ARCO service station and attended to those needs.

As they walked about the station property, Wendy clutched her neck with her left hand. "I feel a little short of breath."

"That's because at higher elevations, the air is different. It's harder to oxygenate the body until you acclimatize to the elevation. People who live here, their bodies tend to produce more hemoglobin to offset that effect," said Sebastian.

"What does hemoglobin have to do with anything?" Wendy asked.

"Hemoglobin carries the oxygen molecules in your bloodstream and distributes them to the tissues in the body. When the tissues don't get enough oxygen distributed to them, lactic acid is produced, which tires the body. This is the basic principle of anaerobic and aerobic exercise. Anaerobic means oxygen debt, like sprinting, whereas aerobic is with proper oxygenation, like long-distance running," replied Sebastian.

"Well, thank you for the science lecture, Mr. Einstein. You have enlightened my day. Now let me enlighten yours."

Wendy then wrapped her arms around Sebastian and placed her lips on his, slipping her tongue in his mouth. Although Sebastian enjoyed it, he didn't like to display affection in public and gently pushed her away with kindness.

Throughout the stop, Spike frolicked around a park next to the service station. There was a creek that he jumped in, cooling off and swimming around. After shaking off, he chased a few squirrels but was unable to score. Spike needed this break; all that time in the car was not good for a sporting breed. When Sebastian called him, he came running over with a T-bone hanging from his mouth that he had found at a picnic site. He was proud of his discovery, displaying his emotion by prancing around, his little stub of a tail wagging back and forth. They got back in the wagon and headed to the Buddhist retreat which was about 33 miles away.

The approach to the retreat was a curvy winding road that hugged the side of a steep mountain. They kept driving up until they reached a plateau and saw a sign with a picture of the Buddha. "Welcome to the Bagwan Retreat," it said. Under the sign was an entrance gate with a guard who was wearing a knee-length white robe. On the side of the guard's left calf was a tattoo of a Buddha with a dagger crossing through his body. Sebastian thought it very strange having this individual at the entrance greeting people.

The guard approached the car. "What can I do for you?" His jet black eyes scanned the visitors.

Sebastian eyed the guard's building from his vantage point and saw an automatic weapon hanging from a hook. Wendy handed the guard her papers.

"Are you excited to finally be at this retreat?" asked Sebastian.

"Yes. At least for a little while." Then she asked the guard if Sebastian and Spike could come with her.

"I'll have to check with Master Bagwan. It won't be long." He went back to his security building, held a phone to his ear, and began to talk.

Wendy turned to Sebastian. "Are you happy to be here with me?"

"Very much so. Yet, this guard gives me the creeps."

Wendy frowned. "He's not exactly Buddhism's answer to Mother Theresa."

Sebastian nodded in agreement and watched as the guard came back.

"They can come in, but the dog is not allowed to run loose." He eyed Wendy. "And there will be extra charges for each of them."

Wendy wrote the payment on a personal check, and the guard lifted up the gate.

Wendy leaned out of the window. "Why do you need a weapon like that?"

"A lot of the local country folks here don't understand the retreat's compassionate and loving nature," he said. "And because we look different, they have, in the past, assaulted some of our people. So now we defend ourselves."

"Oh. I see." Wendy nodded, but Sebastian still thought it didn't jive with the Buddhist scheme.

The guard gave Wendy a color-coded map of the grounds and told her to park in the East parking lot. From there they would have to walk about half a mile to their cottage. The walkway to the living areas was lined with trees, mostly firs and spruce with some large oaks to the sides. As they approached, they began to see people wearing white tops and blue jeans or white robes, and a few were wearing saffron robes. All of the saffron robe wearers had shaved heads, and some of the others did as well.

Sebastian made sure Spike stayed close, as he had been instructed. They approached a row of wooden log cottages, all uniform in shape and size. They looked as if they all came from the same log building company. Wendy found their cottage, and they all entered. It had been a long day, and they were anxious to rest before exploring the retreat.

Just as Wendy and Sebastian were getting comfortable in their sparse yet clean cottage, there was a message over the loudspeaker from Master Bagwan.

"Oh, my blessed children. It is so wonderful that you have graced my presence here at Bagwan Retreat. It is with the most humble of emotions that I tell you I am proud to be here to serve each and every one of you. I look forward to meeting and sharing time with everyone during your stay here. My most respected initiates to the order will be around to make your stay here both enlightened and pleasurable."

A short time later, a man in a saffron robe came to their cottage to inform them of an introductory meeting at the dining hall before dinner. Wendy thanked the man and then asked his name.

"I am nothing but a simple monk whose name is unimportant. Only the Master Bagwan's name is important here."

Upon hearing this, Sebastian felt a chill up his spine. He had studied a bit on the facets of human behavior in groups and knew that some individuals need to find answers not through personal experience but by authoritative domination. People looking to be subservient to another can often be manipulated easily. He didn't want to ruin Wendy's vacation, however, so he just kept his suspicions to himself.

The walk to the dining room was pleasant. They chatted with other campers along the way. The screen door squeaked as they passed through into a huge log hall with two stone fireplaces, wood floors, and high ceilings. There were approximately twenty dining tables, with ten chairs per table, spread geometrically throughout the room. Above each fireplace was a Buddha painting, but the Buddha's face had what Sebastian guessed to be Master Bagwan's countenance.

Once the roughly 180 people had quietly sat at their tables, another monk with a shaved head and wearing a saffron robe greeted everyone with a smile. He said in a monotone voice, "We have certain rules and guidelines that must be followed for the good of everyone. The first is that we practice vegetarianism here at Bagwan

Retreat. The second is the loss of ego: we replace the M in the word *me* with a W. And finally, all personal relationships must be kept on a spiritual level while here at camp."

They all were then served a refreshing fresh fruit salad with tofu and vegetables. Fresh homemade whole wheat bread was also available. Cold, clean mountain water from a local spring was served in chilled glasses.

"I'm starved," cried Wendy in delight as she poured some soy sauce on her meal. "It has been a long day, and this is well deserved."

"I never did thank you for inviting me here. I appreciate it." Sebastian smiled.

"My pleasure," said Wendy as she placed her bare foot under the table and rubbed his crotch gently.

Sebastian could only smile as he nervously looked around.

During the meal, they conversed with several people at their table. Mostly all were novices at the retreat and had no idea of what to expect. They were generally impressed with the grounds and facilities.

Later that evening, they retired to their cottage. Inside was Spike waiting for some personal attention. Wendy had started to really enjoy Spike and was happy to pet him. Sebastian looked around the cottage while they played. There were two single beds, two chests of drawers, and two nightstands. On each nightstand was a hardcover book, *The Esoteric Teachings of Master Bagwan.* The same picture of the Buddha that was above the fireplaces in the dining hall stared back at Sebastian from the books.

Sebastian and Wendy were deep in conversation about their pasts when, all of a sudden, they both thought they heard a distant scream. They silently waited but heard no more, so they put it out of their minds. The whole time, though, Sebastian had an uneasy feeling, like they were being watched. I must be paranoid, he thought. Nothing but pleasantness has occurred so far, so calm down and relax.

The retreat would begin in earnest at the break of dawn, so Wendy gave Sebastian a special kiss goodnight, and they both went to sleep in separate beds.

The sun was just beginning to show its morning face when the loudspeaker tweaked and a soothing voice said, "This is Master

Bagwan. Good morning to all. I trust that you slept well and are now getting ready for morning yoga practices. Our initiates will lead you in the courtyard in ten minutes." The loudspeaker then went dead.

The morning was filled with different classes, some more esoteric than others. They learned some breathing exercises and the history of Buddhism, which began in India with the teachings of Gautoma Buddha before spreading to all of Asia.

During one of the classes, an initiate asked Wendy, "What are the Four Noble Truths?"

"They are the path to salvation," replied Wendy.

"Very good answer, but can you tell me specifically what they are?"

"The first is suffering, the second is uprising or craving, the third is cessation, and the fourth is following the eightfold path, which is proper view, proper intention, proper speech, proper action, proper livelihood, proper effort, proper mindfulness, and proper concentration," said Wendy.

"That was an excellent answer. Let's all give her the recognition she deserves."

Everyone got up and gave her a hug. Wendy was beaming, and Sebastian was proud of his new friend. The initiate monk then went on to teach about the forms of Buddhism, including Hinayana Buddhism and Mayahana Buddhism.

The morning was intense and everybody was ready for a lunch break. They all went to the dining hall and sat at the same tables as before, except this time they sat with new acquaintances rather than strangers. They were served brown rice and black beans with eggplant soufflé casserole and pieces of fresh fruit. During lunch the group had jovial discussions, and laughter was plentiful. It was a pleasant meal.

Sebastian was anxious to get back to the cottage to see Spike and let him get some exercise. Spike was extremely happy to see them both. They had an hour before the programs began again, so they decided to explore.

As they walked past a group of cottages just like theirs, they both waved to the other campers. They continued on past an older building which Sebastian assumed housed the initiate monks. Spike led the way as they continued down the road. Sebastian and Wendy took turns throwing Spike's ball, which Spike would retrieve. They were happily distracted and did not see the sign that said OFF LIMITS.

The three had walked another five or ten minutes down the road when Sebastian saw a garage with an open padlock. He walked over to take a look.

Wendy said, "Do you think we really should?"

Sebastian laughed. "No learning ever took place without following one's curiosity." He opened the door and turned to Wendy. "You won't believe what's in here."

Wendy walked over and saw two Silver Ghost Rolls Royce automobiles, one gray and one white. She blurted out, "Somebody is not following the Eightfold Path!"

They continued walking and discovered a beautiful home of wood, glass, stone, and steel. It perfectly blended with the environment. Sebastian thought that it could have been designed by Frank Lloyd Wright. As they were admiring the home, a Jeep pulled up and a dark-complected security guard with a beard jumped out. In his hands was an automatic weapon.

"What are you doing here?" Without waiting for an answer, he pushed Sebastian. "Get the f--k outta here and don't come back."

Sebastian and Wendy didn't waste time. They turned to hurry back, but Spike started growling at the guard.

"Spike! Come here. Now!" Sebastian yelled.

The man pointed his weapon at Spike with his finger on the trigger.

"Spike!" Sebastian yelled again.

Wendy grabbed Sebastian's arm and they both held their breath.

Finally, Spike came running back to Sebastian, and the three hurried back to the retreat.

Wendy was shaking, and tears streamed down her cheeks. Sebastian tried to console her, but his nerves were on edge, too.

"I don't know what, but something strange and malevolent is taking place around here," said Sebastian.

"What just happened?" Wendy asked.

Sebastian shook his head, unsure what to say.

Wendy faced him. "Do you think. . . ?"

Sebastian took her hand. "I don't know what's going on, Wendy, but I think we should keep quiet about what just happened."

She nodded and sighed. "I have been so looking forward to this retreat."

Before she could start crying again, Sebastian led her back to the cottage to get cleaned up.

They finished the afternoon programs, ate a fast dinner, and spent the evening at their cottage trying to relax after the stressful day. Sebastian was throwing the ball for Spike in the cottage, when Spike jumped for the ball and knocked the picture off the wall. Sebastian went to put it back and saw a small peephole in the wall big enough for a camera lens, but he saw no camera. Sebastian waved Wendy out to the porch where he told her about the peephole. They decided they would leave the next day, but only if the timing was right. That night while lying in bed, not able to sleep well because of what had happened that day and the light of the full moon, they heard muffled sounds from the cottage nearby. They looked out the window and saw three men carrying a young woman with long blonde hair. One man's hand was over her mouth as she was quickly whisked away into a van.

"Did you see what I saw?" said Wendy.

"Most definitely." Sebastian nodded.

At breakfast the next morning, they saw that the young woman from their table was missing. They inquired as to her whereabouts, and someone said she had gotten sick and went home. Wendy and Sebastian looked at each other, excused themselves, and went back to the cottage. Sebastian let Spike out while they gathered their belongings. Ten minutes later, Sebastian saw Spike digging a hole at the far end of a field by the trees at the edge of the retreat grounds. He called Spike, but the dog kept digging. Finally, Spike came running with a bone in his mouth.

"Oh my God," cried Sebastian.

"What's the matter?" asked Wendy.

"Spike, come here." Sebastian took the bone from Spike's mouth as the dog's tail wagged. He held up the bone for Wendy to see. "That is a human humerus bone."

Wendy looked at him, questioning.

"It's the upper arm bone."

Wendy wrapped her arms around herself, holding tight to her

own upper arms. "Are you sure?"

Sebastian nodded. "It must have been buried out there. Who knows what else is happening here. We are getting out of this place right now. Quick. Throw me your keys, grab your bag, and let's make a dash for the car."

As they hurried to the car, they heard a voice yell, "You can't leave now."

They were out of breath, but the adrenaline was flowing. The three jumped in the car and sped toward the exit. When a guard came out in the road motioning them to stop, Sebastian floored the accelerator and rammed the gate, shattering it in a hundred pieces. Still shaking, they drove to the nearest town and contacted law enforcement.

Sebastian went to the Colorado State Police office, told them his story, and showed them the bone. The police told him that he and Wendy should stick around town; they would be needed as witnesses for the prosecution. The police gathered reinforcements and a warrant, called for the SWAT team, and then went and raided the Bagwan compound.

When the police approached the compound, they were met with gunfire. The police hunkered down and called in the tactical squadron. Ten minutes later, two troop-carrying helicopters swooped in and dispatched a trained assault team. Tear gas was launched into the retreat buildings while other police officers helped get the campers and innocent monks off the retreat property. After several hours of standoff and armed conflict, Master Bagwan and his followers surrendered. Immediately after, sniffing dogs and a highly trained forensics expert from Dallas, Texas, were brought in. Forensics, a new science, was just beginning to develop as a legal framework that could be used in a court of law.

The front page of the *Colorado Springs Dispatch* the next day read:

SPRINGER SPANIEL EXPOSES A CULT
An English springer spaniel named Spike uncovered the bone of one of many murder and rape victims at a sinister compound posing as a benevolent Buddhist retreat. State Police responded to the evidence with enough force to subdue and capture the armed criminals. . . .

It continued with a full three-page story with pictures of the compound. Reporters from all across the United States came to interview Wendy and Sebastian, but it was Spike who got all the attention and picture publicity. Even the mayor came by to see Spike, bringing a bagful of dog treats.

"I understand you'll be staying with us for a few days to give your full testimony," he said to Sebastian as he petted Spike.

Sebastian nodded.

"We'd like to set you up at the Holiday Inn, free of charge, as a thank you for your service to our community." He scratched Spike's ears. "And you, little guy. We'd be honored if you would lead our Independence Day parade next week."

He looked up to Sebastian and Wendy.

"Of course," Sebastian said. "Spike would love it."

On July 4th, Spike was dressed in an American flag with red and blue puff balls on each ear. All the schoolchildren wanted to play with Spike. He was content with the attention and all the treats he was getting. During all the activity, Wendy and Sebastian were grateful to be free of the retreat and have a few days together before they went their separate ways.

Chapter 5

Sebastian was sorry to see Wendy leave, but he knew that's the way it must be sometimes. He knew it was important to enjoy every moment in the moment. One can never hold on to an experience except in a memory. And a memory can never do it justice. He waved goodbye as he tucked a paper with her phone number and address in his pocket. Spike just watched her leave from his vantage point on Route 50 in Cañon City. The travelers got a few uneventful rides into Salida and through some beautiful country near Gunnison. In Montrose, they picked up some grub. As they were walking through town, they heard a voice.

"What do you think you're doing?" said a law enforcement officer in a city patrol car.

"I'm just walking here enjoying the day, officer," Sebastian replied.

"Well, you can just keep walking another mile or two right out of town. We don't want the likes of you here, and we don't allow hitchhiking, either."

"Okay, I get your point; we are not here to make any trouble."

"Good, 'cause I'm not in the mood for any."

Sebastian and Spike walked to the town limits with the police car right behind escorting them. The policeman parked his car and waited and watched. The day was retreating quickly. Sebastian looked at his map, which showed barren country and a stretch of desert ahead after they arrived in Grand Junction. He thought they would try and get one more ride into Utah, and then settle down for the night.

They waited a little while, the whole time the policeman

watching. When a light green pickup truck started slowing down, Sebastian examined the driver. He must have been 270 pounds. What then caught Sebastian's eye were the two rifles secured on the back window.

Holy shit, this could be really bad, Sebastian thought. He might take me out in the desert and blow me away.

The country at the time was divided between long-haired anti-war protesters and love-it-or-leave-it American patriots. Even though most Americans were in the gray area between, Sebastian knew that he might be initially seen as the former and a fair-game target. He glanced at the police officer and approached the truck.

"Where you going?" said the driver.

"We are heading to the coast," replied Sebastian.

"I can take you as far as Green River, Utah."

"That sounds pretty good to me."

"What are you doing along this road?" the man asked.

Sebastian knew that the best defense was a good offense, so he immediately tried to become this man's friend. He figured it's harder to kill somebody you like.

"I'm Sebastian and this is Spike." He gave the springer spaniel a pat. "We are on a trip to see the U.S.A."

The man nodded. "My name is Bill. I live in Green River. I was working in Colorado this week doing civil engineering for the federal government."

The two shook hands and acknowledged each other with a smile. Bill wore yellow rimmed glasses and had a small turned up nose. To the right of his mouth was a streak of brown stain from the drippings of chewing tobacco that had leaked from the wad in his right cheek. His brown hair curled out from under a green and white John Deere hat exposing the shaved part around the sides and back. He wore a blue work shirt and blue denim jeans. His belly hung over, hiding his belt buckle. His large brown work boots were resting on the gas and clutch pedals. Bill smiled, revealing poor dentition, including some nasty cavities and missing spaces.

"Aren't you scared hitchhiking around the country like this?" he asked as he took a swig of Coke.

"Should I be?" Sebastian checked to see if the door was unlocked.

"I should think so. This is not the friendly place of our forefathers anymore."

"Sometimes you can't let fear guide you and hold you back from doing what you want to do," said Sebastian.

"You do have a point." Bill nodded. "In fact, I admire you for it." He spat tobacco juice out the window.

The two got along surprisingly well. Bill gave Sebastian a brief history of the area, pointing out Indian caves and explaining some of the petroglyphs. Working as an engineer, Bill spent a lot of time in remote areas, especially in the national parks and territories. He gained quite a bit of knowledge that's not in books. While Bill drove, Sebastian opened a can of sardines. Bill looked at it with a little desire, so Sebastian offered him some. What had started out as a fearful ride now had Sebastian feeding Bill sardines as he drove. Sebastian took each sardine, one by one, held it over Bill's face and dropped it in his mouth. Bill tucked the wad of tobacco in his upper cheek as he swallowed each sardine. And all the while, Spike rode in the bed of the pickup. He liked the breeze in his face as he leaned out the side behind the passenger window.

"Is this your kid?" asked Sebastian, as he pointed to a picture on the dashboard.

"Yep. That's my oldest boy, Kenny. He's thirteen years old. I've also got a ten-year-old named Jenny, and an eight-year-old named Lenny."

"Is your wife named Penny?" asked Sebastian.

"How did you know that?"

"Let's just say I got lucky."

The sun was beginning to set behind the mountains, leaving a pinkish-blue cover over the landscape. The sun would jut in at certain points, acting as a spotlight on the desert rock formations around the cliffs.

"So where do you stay on the road?" asked Bill.

"If there is a campground nearby, I try to stay there. If not, I just put up a tent and crawl into my sleeping bag on the side of the road."

"There is a KOA campground in Green River, but they'll be closed by the time we get there."

"That's even better. I can walk in, take a shower, use the restroom, sleep, get up at the crack of dawn and leave. Nobody ever knew I was there. When you don't have much money, you find ways to get by," said Sebastian.

Bill had finished drinking his soda and was feeling full in the bladder. He pulled over to take a leak, saying he would be back in a minute. Sebastian acknowledged and also got out to urinate. Bill was at the front end of the truck, and Sebastian was at the back, both watering the landscape. Even Spike was adding his share. Just as Bill was about to finish, he heard a rattle. He couldn't see, but he had a hunch it was the unmistakable sound of a western rattlesnake. He clumsily rushed to get all zipped and out of there. Suddenly, Spike pounced on the snake. He had the snake just below the head, shaking and biting it. He didn't stop until the snake went limp.

"Your dog just saved my marriage," said Bill as he tightened his belt. "If he didn't get that rattler, my wife would have had a lot of lonely nights."

Sebastian came running over, making sure that Spike hadn't gotten bit and was all right. He appeared to be and was wagging his tail, happy to be of service.

Bill said, "For that brave deed, you two need to be rewarded."

Sebastian shook his head. "That's not necessary. We are grateful for the ride."

"Nonsense. It's done. The two of you will spend the night at my house with my family. My kids will love meeting Spike. However, our cat, Prissy, probably won't. We have a spare bedroom. You can clean up, eat, and be on your way tomorrow."

They pulled into a paved asphalt driveway after 10 p.m. It was littered with bicycles, basketballs, and roller skates. The headlights showed an aluminum-sided ranch home with an antenna atop the chimney. Beside the driveway was a flower garden in full bloom.

As Bill opened the front door, he yelled, "Honey, I hope you are dressed, 'cause we have company."

Sebastian could hear the scurrying of two females running to the bathroom to freshen up.

"This is Sebastian. And his dog Spike. They are going to stay the night with us. Spike here saved Big Joe from a deadly rattlesnake tonight. I was out takin' a leak, just about to shake Big Joe off, when this rattler, who had other ideas, was killed by Spike."

Bill turned to Sebastian. "I'm sorry. I didn't introduce you to my family. This is my wife, Penny, and my kids, Kenny, Jenny, and Lenny."

Penny was eyeing this long-curly-haired, bearded young man with a backpack. "How did you guys get together?" She looked between them.

"Spike and I are traveling the country on foot, experiencing life, and your husband was gracious enough to give us a lift and help us along the way."

"Well, any friend of my husband's is a friend of mine, so make yourself right at home. Are you hungry?"

"Actually, very much so. A peanut butter and jelly sandwich would be just fine."

"Is that all you want? We've got all kinds of fruit, chips, ice cream. You just help yourself."

Sebastian went and made his PBJ sandwich and took an apple. He then gave Spike a bowl of his food. As Sebastian sat at the table, the kids encircled Spike, eager to play with him. He also heard a hiss from the corner. It was Prissy, a white Persian cat, its back curved with hair standing up.

"Don't worry about her. She's all show. She looks worse than she acts. She is actually quite adorable once she settles down," said Penny.

In the meantime, Spike kept his distance from the cat. Sebastian observed a neatly decorated living room and kitchen. There was a cargo-type wooden sofa with pillows and a La-Z-Boy armchair. The chair had been worn in the seat, from years of shouldering Bill's 270 pounds Sebastian surmised. Above the stone fireplace were antlers from deer and elk. Across the living room, above the sofa was a hawk and the head of a black bear. Both had been keenly stuffed by a taxidermist. The little knickknacks that littered the shelves in the kitchen and family room were an eclectic group from roadside galleries and flea market bazaars. The house had a warm feeling, and he and Spike were content to spend the night there. They stayed up a couple of hours in conversation. Sebastian mostly listened, as Penny seemed to monopolize the conversation. Sebastian let her, figuring that she spent most of her life with the kids and had few opportunities to converse with an outsider adult. She went on about how she and Bill met and the delivery of her children, amongst other domestic happenings. While she spoke, Sebastian sensed that she was someone who truly behaved in a spiritual way with a true spirit whether she went to church or not. By the end of the night, Sebastian felt like a long-lost cousin. They finally said goodnight. She hugged Sebastian and Spike, Bill shook his hand, and they all went to bed.

Up at the crack of dawn, Sebastian showered, got his pack together, ate, and said goodbye. He left a little poem on the bed.

> Blessings occur when least expected
> God lends a hand
> Even when not seemingly connected
> The fact that we have met
> Is no mere coincidence
> That angels housed a man and his pet

On his way to work, Bill dropped Sebastian and Spike off in Green River, Utah, by Interstate 70. Once again, they were on the road.

Chapter 6

Sebastian and Spike sat by the roadside for a couple of hours. The sun was starting to rise, along with the Fahrenheit degrees. Luckily, they had just imbibed some water and filled the canteen. Sebastian was stroking the top of Spike's head when an old red and white Ford pickup stopped. The driver asked where they were going. Sebastian answered out West, and the driver told him to hop in.

As Sebastian slid into the passenger's seat, he noticed the man was in his late twenties, was of American Indian heritage, and wore an Indian-style headband keeping his long, fine, black hair off his face. Covering his chest was a tie-dyed t-shirt with the words Grateful Dead on the front. On his left wrist, he had a silver and turquoise bracelet that had various inscriptions on it. His blue jeans were faded, and he wore no belt. On his feet were a pair of handmade moccasins of what looked like tan suede. His hands showed no calluses.

"How you doing, Kemosabe?" the man asked.

"We are doing pretty well, especially now that you picked us up. My name is Sebastian and this is Spike."

"What kind of trip are the two of you on?"

"We are out to see the country and hope to gain a little insight along the way."

"My name is John. I'm heading through southern Utah and into northern Arizona. You are welcome to come with me. I know a little bit about this part of the country, and you can get a guided tour, free of charge."

"Sounds good to me. By the way, I noticed you called me Kemosabe earlier, like Tonto used to call the Lone Ranger in the television show. What does that mean anyway?"

"Caucasian asshole," John replied.

Sebastian quickly turned, quite surprised by the answer. John was smiling.

"I'm just messing with you. I like to shock people sometimes. It's fun."

"Okay. The laugh's on me. It was pretty funny."

"Actually, I don't know what Kemosabe means, probably some made-up TV name."

Driving down Route 70 to Route 89, John took Sebastian and Spike on two-lane roads through the Dixie National Forest and then through Bryce Canyon National Park. They had many great views of the park. They observed fantastic rock formations, rising like phallic symbols reaching for the sun. These hoodoos are quite a sight, especially with the sun and shadows playing peek-a-boo throughout the canyon. They stopped so Sebastian could take pictures. He had John and Spike stand next to the ledge with the hoodoos in the background. Farther out, along the top of the escarpment, they gazed at wondrous rock formations of spires and arches. Then they approached and viewed the rock formations in the Queen's Garden.

After spending a few hours in Bryce, they drove about fifty miles to Zion National Park. Sebastian thought this park was even more spectacular than Bryce Canyon. The truck approached Zion from the bottom. In Bryce, the road was on the top of the canyon, but in Zion the spectacular cliffs towered over the road below. The route had numerous S-curves, which switched back up the mountain, giving the rider different views of the park. They could see the wondrous cliffs of Navajo sandstone, created by years of erosion from the Virgin River. They viewed the prominent features of the park, such as the Altar of Sacrifice, Angels Landing, and the Temple of Sinawava.

Leaving Utah, they followed Route 89 and eventually came into the Navajo Nation in northern Arizona. True to his word, John continued the guided tour, telling Sebastian about each place they passed, including the Monument Valley Park and the Navajo National Monument. Sebastian was able to see Betatakin, the ancient living area of the Anasazi people. John explained that Betatakin means "ledge house" and that the Anasazi had lived in houses built literally into the cliffs. Sebastian was in awe.

"I want to bring you to the village where I grew up. It's not far from here. But first, there is an area that I used to explore as a teenager, just outside my village."

They drove about twenty-five miles, turned onto a rocky road, and stopped by some unusual rock formations. They exited the truck, and Spike happily ran around. John led the way behind the rocks to an entrance to what appeared to be a cave.

"You don't have any phobias about exploring caves, do you?" asked John.

"No. I quite enjoy trying and seeing new things."

John pulled a flashlight out of his pocket, bent over, and entered the 5-by-3-foot entrance. Sebastian and Spike followed. They walked about forty feet and gazed at a wall. There were pictures painted on the wall of deer, sheep, and bears. Next to the animals were images of Navajo warriors, bows drawn, ready to shoot arrows. To the right was a picture of heavenly bodies—the sun, the moon, and some star formations.

"These were here when I was a kid," John said. "My ancestors supposedly drew these centuries ago. Over here, I wrote my name when I was eight years old." John shined his light on some Navajo writing.

"What does that say?" asked Sebastian.

"It says Runs with Lightning."

"That's your name?" questioned Sebastian. "Why?"

"The story is told that when my mother was about to deliver me, it was during a tremendous lightning storm. All the midwives were there helping my mother when a bolt of lightning hit our hut of rock, logs, and dirt. No one was hurt, but I was delivered within minutes of that lightning bolt. So that became my Navajo given name."

Just as John finished the last word, they heard a loud grinding noise. The two turned and saw a boulder fall and cover most of the entrance to the cave. "Oh shit!" they both exclaimed in unison. They ran to the entrance. Only a small opening was left at the bottom. John tried to move the boulder first, and then Sebastian tried, but to no avail. John then attempted to squeeze through the opening, but his shoulders were too wide. He was smaller than Sebastian, so Sebastian didn't bother trying. Many four letter words were then repeated in the next few minutes.

"I have an idea," said John.

"I sure hope it's a good one, because nobody knows we are in here."

"I've got this journal in my pocket. Let's write a note asking for help and pin it on Spike's collar. Do you think he can fit through?"

"He may be able to, with a little help from us," said Sebastian.

John wrote a note explaining who he was and what cave they were in.

"Tell them to bring a 4x4 truck with a winch to pull that boulder out," said Sebastian.

Sebastian secured the finished note to Spike's collar and said to Spike, "Buddy, if ever in your life you had to retrieve something, now is the time. Go find help." He then pushed Spike out the hole, hoping he would understand what was needed, and not just lay down outside the cave.

"We might be here a long time, and we don't have any food and water," said John.

"The best thing we can do now is just relax and not waste too much energy pacing around," said Sebastian. "Why don't you give me a better understanding of the Navajo people? Like their concept of the universe, their basis for religion, family relationships, and anything else that meets your fancy. I mean, it's not like we are on a tight schedule here. Wait, before you do that, tell me about yourself. You seem too cosmopolitan to have lived on the reservation your whole life."

They settled in, sitting with their backs against the wall.

"I did grow up not far from here and learned the Navajo way of life, but my father knew that I had greater comprehension of academia than most of the other children. He wanted me to get an education, knowing full-well that the path of the American Indian was leading down a dead end road, unless we get educated. He worked many jobs, scraping together enough money so I could go to a private school, which later led to my achieving a college degree."

"Your father had a great deal of insight."

"He most certainly did. In fact, whenever the tribal council needed advice before they made an important decision, they would often call on my father for his wisdom."

"Did your siblings go to private school, also?"

"No, they didn't take to book learning like I did. They were happy to be involved with agriculture and hands-on apprenticeships."

"Where did you go to college?"

"I got my bachelor's degree from Arizona State and then received my Ph.D. from the University of Chicago School of Economics."

"What do you plan to do with your specialized education?" asked Sebastian.

"I would like to give back to the Navajo people. I want to organize profitable business ventures on the reservation that would give dignified work and income to all in the tribe who want it."

"What kind of businesses do you have in mind?"

"It's not fully formulated yet, but for starters mining, tourism, lines of clothing, and possibly a gambling casino. It hasn't been tried yet, but watching Las Vegas grow has given me hope."

Sebastian nodded. The two sat quietly for a few moments.

"John, do you believe in God?" Sebastian asked.

John looked at Sebastian quietly before answering. "That depends on what you mean by God. If you are asking do I believe in Jesus Christ or Mohammed or Buddha, the answer is no. Now, if you mean the cosmogony of the universe and the meaning of all the planets and stars. Or that many animals were created to assist us in harmony, then the answer is yes. Many of the Navajo believe that with physical death, the person is left behind, and the body of the deceased joins the rest of the universe. In general, my people do not believe in an afterlife, and do not believe in immortality. Of course, there is much more to our beliefs than I can explain now.

"What about you, Sebastian. What do you believe in?"

"I'm not quite sure. I don't believe in these man-made religions with all their rituals, but I think there may be some sort of order in the universe. The idea of reincarnation seems plausible to me, because some people are born so intelligent, with a very high consciousness, and others are so primitive and unenlightened. My basic concept for living can be summed up in one word: LOVE. If you have love in your soul, and do not ever mean harm to anyone, and try to be the best human being you can be, then I believe you are headed in the right direction. Does that make any sense to you?"

"You sound like an agent for Paul McCartney—'All You Need Is Love.'"

They both started laughing.

"Here we are laughing, and for all we know, this might be the last place we see," said John.

"Are there any other exits out of this cave?" inquired Sebastian.

"No. When I was young we looked but never found any." John leaned his head back against the wall and closed his eyes.

Sebastian studied the images painted in the cave. "How long have the Navajo people been here in this territory?"

"Many say that it could be anywhere from 500 to 700 years. Legend has it that my people migrated from northern Canada to the Plains and then down to the Southwest. We were originally a nomadic people who hunted, but after coming in contact with the Spanish, we acquired horses. We also learned agriculture from the Pueblo people and silverwork from the Mexicans. Many of these contacts shaped our civilization as it is today. We pretty much lived our own lives until we came head-to-head with Manifest Destiny."

"Do you think your people could have done anything different?"

"Not much. Two totally different civilizations collided, one hell-bent on getting its way and willing to destroy anything in its path, the other unable or unwilling to adapt quickly enough to keep its integrity and known lifestyle."

The two talked for hours discussing everything from history, politics, and family to their personal last wishes. The light from the small entrance opening began to dim, and then disappear. It was nightfall and still no help had arrived. The cave climate was comfortable, even on the cool side. Sebastian hoped that it was cool enough to prevent snakes from slithering around. The two finally fell asleep.

They awoke in the morning, when sunlight could be seen through the small entrance hole. Thirst and hunger were beginning to gnaw at their personal comfort. Sebastian attempted to move the boulder, but was woefully physically inadequate for the task. He then tried searching the cave for another exit, but soon learned that John's experience was correct. Things were not looking good. The day began to get warmer, and Sebastian could feel his strength beginning to ebb.

All of a sudden, they heard a noise.

"Did you hear something?" said John, as he jumped to his feet.

"I thought so, but I'm not sure," said Sebastian.

Then they both heard barking and the sound of a vehicle approaching.

"That sounds like Spike, and I hear voices, but it's not English. Is that Navajo?" said Sebastian.

"It is remnants of the Athabascan language, the language of the Navajo and Apache ancestors. It sounds as if Spike was able to reach my tribal people after all."

They heard someone say loudly, in broken English, "Are you in there, okay?"

John and Sebastian started yelling loudly, telling the person to move the boulder blocking the entrance. The man said that they couldn't get a truck with a winch to the entrance of the cave, but they had a jackhammer. Someone climbed up on the rocks above the boulder and began to jackhammer through the rock. The noise reverberated off the cliffs and was deafening inside the cave. This went on for a couple of hours until, finally, they broke through the rock, splitting it in half. It then fell to the ground outside the cave. Spike ran in and licked Sebastian's face. The Navajos were hugging their friend and relative, Runs With Lightning. They had a canteen of water in the vehicle, which John and Sebastian quickly drank. The group was ecstatic and were all congratulating Spike for his major part in the rescue operation.

One of the rescuers approached Sebastian. "You must come to our village and join in the celebration as our guest. Your dog is welcome, too. In the true Navajo tradition, he assisted us in the rescue of one our community's finest citizens, Runs with Lightning."

Sebastian smiled and nodded. "Thank you. I have always wanted to experience an American Indian celebration."

The ride to the village was wonderful. Spike laid across Sebastian's lap—he didn't want him out of his presence. John was very pleased with the rescue and that his people had embraced him so dearly. As they arrived, many villagers came out of their homes and welcomed them warmly. Sebastian, not knowing Navajo custom, was a little shy, not wanting to offend anyone by being too forward or friendly.

Once the other Navajos heard of the rescue, they came from many miles to see Runs With Lightning and the dog that saved the day. Spike was treated with much honor. Sebastian, being Spike's master, was given honorary status as a deserved guest of the Navajo people. That night, quite a celebration took place, with dancing, chants, delicious foods made from corn, flour, lamb, and different vegetables and herbs. They passed around drinks derived from the agave plant. Sebastian soon found himself getting quite intoxicated, not only from the drink, but also from the celebration itself.

"What are they celebrating now?" Sebastian said to John.

"We are celebrating the rise of the Navajo people from the underworlds to our present world, where first man and woman prepared the world for the coming of the Navajo," replied John.

"I notice that everyone is wearing such vibrant colors. Do the colors each have different meanings?"

"Yes. In Navajo cosmogony, colors are often associated with different meanings—white with purity, red with war. The whole concept has some similarities to many other metaphysical beliefs of different religions around the world."

After hours of celebrating, Sebastian found himself having a personal religious experience. He saw images of God and heard Him talking to him, telling him that he had reached the pinnacle of spirituality. He kept repeating, "That's right. I'm there." Later, of course, Sebastian realized it was the effects of mescal that had led him to have an out-of-body hallucinatory experience. This, combined with the American Indian spiritual celebration, might have led to a life-changing experience for any young man.

The campfire and celebration continued into the wee hours. Sebastian was getting tired and asked John where they were going to sleep.

"We can go to my mother's house. She said earlier that you and Spike would be welcome to stay. In fact, she insisted on it. She is so happy that Spike was instrumental in my rescue that nothing you asked would be an inconvenience."

"Will your father be there?"

"I'm afraid not. He died from pneumonia when I was 22 years old. At least he was alive to see me graduate college. I think that was one of the happiest days of his life. He was so proud of me. I will always try to honor his memory."

The two went to John's mother's house and, after talking for a while with his mom, they went to bed.

It was late in the morning when Sebastian awakened. Spike was laying by his side. He didn't remember much from the night before and had no memory of coming to this home. It was a very small home, simple but clean. His friend John was still asleep on a couch across the room, while Sebastian had been sleeping atop blankets on the floor. The wood walls were decorated with oil paintings of the Southwest landscape. Interspersed between were a few pictures of Navajo children and a large black-and-white picture of a Navajo man and woman in what appeared to be a wedding photograph. Their smiles were sincere, yet subdued. In a corner of the room stood an old metal frame bed with a Navajo woven blanket. In another corner was a small refrigerator and a wood-burning stove. Trinkets dotted the window sills. On one was a five-inch Statue of Liberty and a picture of John F. Kennedy.

"It's about time you finally got up," Sebastian said to John.

"How long have you been awake?" John replied, yawning.

"Just long enough to realize I've really got to use the bathroom. Where is it?"

"Go out back. It's about thirty yards behind the hogan."

When Sebastian came back through the door, Runs with Lightning's mother was speaking with her son in Athabascan. Her facial expressions reflected the delight of having her beloved child home once again. She was very short and had tough, wrinkled skin. Her gray hair was pulled back and twisted into two braids. She wore a tan cotton dress with turquoise, red, and white decorations. On each ear hung long silver and turquoise earrings shaped like the sun and moon. White and turquoise beads were wrapped around her neck. Her feet were covered in moccasins similar to John's. Smiling, she grabbed Sebastian's hands. He could feel the warmth of her personality filtering through his fingers. In broken English, she thanked him for bringing her boy home and asked him to stay awhile as her guest. Sebastian thanked her for her kindness.

Sebastian and Spike went for a walk around the village, receiving friendly smiles from just about everyone they passed. It is a very strange feeling being here, Sebastian thought. Not just a different location, but a very dramatic cultural change. After walking for a while, he headed back to John's mother's house. John was outside, and he called to Sebastian.

"How would you like to do some work?"

"What do you want me to do?" answered Sebastian.

"The fences need shoring up, and some of the men are going out to repair them, or the sheep and cattle may cause accidents on the highway. I'll give you a hammer and some nails, gloves, and wire. We will drop you off, and you will work your way back to the group."

"I'll be glad to. I can bring Spike, too."

Later, at the roadside fence, Sebastian was working, wearing a bandanna across his forehead and bending over. A Chevrolet convertible full of white teenagers drove slowly by.

One of the kids started yelling, "You f—kin' Indian prick. Where's your buffalo?" and another one hurled an empty beer bottle that just missed Sebastian's head.

Sebastian shook his head as the car roared away. The young generation, he thought, has inherited their elders' prejudices just as they had from their elders and so on back through history. Sebastian's heart broke for the community of his new friends.

Sebastian worked for several more hours. He was getting very thirsty, and Spike was panting heavily. Finally seeing the others, he was relieved that they had completed their task. Everyone piled into the back of the pickup and drove back to the village. Sebastian was glad that he had been able to give something back to the Navajos since they had been so gracious with their hospitality.

As Sebastian was getting his fill of water, John came up to tell him that some of his people were performing Navajo heritage dancing and selling tapes at the South Rim of the Grand Canyon.

"It's quite a sight to see. If you would like, they have room for you and Spike in their pickup. From there it will be easy to catch a ride to Las Vegas and farther west."

"That would be nice. I've always wanted to view the Grand Canyon."

"Good. I will inform them, but we must feed you a nice meal before you leave. My mother is making you a special Pueblo recipe."

After eating, Sebastian and Spike gave their goodbyes and continued their journey west. Sebastian had a strong feeling that Runs with Lightning would someday change the Navajo future with his leadership and knowledge.

Chapter 7

Sebastian stayed and watched the Navajos perform their dancing for a while by Angel's Lodge at the South Rim of the Grand Canyon. He then gave all a warm embrace and thanked them for the ride to America's grandest natural spectacle.

The afternoon was warm and clear, but clouds could be seen on the horizon. They were now in a U.S. National Park, so Sebastian had to keep Spike on a leash or risk being ejected from the area. Not used to being secured, Spike was continuously tugging and pulling Sebastian rather than walking by his side. Sebastian was getting a wee bit irritated with Spike. He just wanted to quietly and peacefully enjoy the majestic landscape of the canyon.

Once again, his arm was yanked by his 55-pound springer spaniel.

"Spike, will you quit pulling," yelled Sebastian.

Spike continued with increased force and respirations.

"What do you want?" shouted a thoroughly annoyed Sebastian.

Finally, Sebastian turned around and saw a little puppy playing by a tent in the nearby campground. Hopeless, he gave in and walked Spike over to the puppy. The little puppy, which looked like a young border collie, was all over Spike. Spike wasn't but a couple of years older and was happy to have a playmate for a while.

"What's all the commotion?" said a voice from the tent.

"My dog's just playing with your puppy," replied Sebastian.

An attractive blonde-haired, blue-eyed female in her early twenties, came out from the tent and introduced herself as Rita. She was about 5 feet 9 inches tall, wore a low-cut pink blouse with no sleeves, cut-off blue jean shorts, and sandals. A pink and blue necklace circled her neck.

"Do you like my new puppy? She's only twelve weeks old."

"What's his name?" asked Sebastian.

"I've named her Lady Luck."

"I'm sorry. I didn't look at the underside yet," Sebastian laughed.

"Who are you? And what are you doing here?" asked Rita as she buttoned up her shirt.

"I'm Sebastian and this is Spike. We just arrived here a few hours ago, and then Spike noticed Lady Luck."

"Where are you staying?" asked Rita.

"Nowhere yet. I hadn't really thought about it."

"I don't mean to be pushy, but you better think about it soon. These campgrounds fill up very quickly. If you don't find a place soon, you might be S.O.L., if you know what I mean."

"Are you here with anybody else?" asked Sebastian.

"No. I was supposed to have a girlfriend, but she got called into work at the last minute. I really wanted to get away for a couple of days, so here I am."

"There is plenty of grass here. Could I pitch my tent by yours?" asked Sebastian.

Rita thought for a moment and then nodded. "Lady Luck could use a friend, and you don't seem like somebody that I should be afraid of. Given that, I guess it would be all right if you shared my campground site."

"Thank you. I really didn't know the deal on this campground, and you just made my day," Sebastian said with a smile.

"Actually, I was thinking more about Spike and Lady Luck than you."

Sebastian set up his tent, filled Spike's bowl with water, gave him some dry dog food, and they were good to go. The afternoon gave way to evening as Rita and Sebastian casually got to know each other.

"Did you travel a great distance to get here?" asked Sebastian.

"Not too far. I live in Las Vegas, Nevada."

"What kind of work do you do there?"

"I work at the Flamingo Hotel. I'm a dealer. I usually do blackjack, but sometimes it's stud poker."

"By looking at you, I never would have guessed that you would be a casino dealer."

"Why not? It pays well, the tips are great, and I get a break every hour. Plus, our benefits have been consistently improving. Have you ever been to Vegas?"

"No, but I'm always open to new experiences."

"People have a mistaken idea of Vegas. Sure, there are pimps, prostitutes, and mafia, but there's also a lot of really good people there who see nothing morally wrong with gambling and who like a fast life. No doubt about it, Las Vegas will thrive."

Sebastian and Rita were getting along well. She was very curious about how he could just hitchhike with a dog and not be afraid.

"Sometimes you just have to forge ahead and hope for the best."

"Sebastian, why didn't you just drive out here?" asked Rita.

"That would have made my life easier, I suppose, but I don't have a car or the money to operate one. Besides, this way I get to meet interesting people that I would not have if I had a car."

"But isn't it dangerous out there?"

"I try not to think about the negative too much," replied Sebastian.

Rita was warming up to Sebastian. When she talked, she would touch him on the hand or elbow. She kept fixing her hair, pushing it off her face. She leaned in toward him as they talked. Spike was great, but Sebastian was happy to have human companionship, especially from such an attractive woman.

Rita wasn't wearing a brassiere, and as the sun set, the chill in the air made her nipples firm against her blouse.

"It's getting a little chilly. I think I'll get a sweatshirt," said Rita.

Rita went to her tent and came back out with a light blue hooded sweatshirt with pink letters on the front that said LAS VEGAS MY KIND OF TOWN.

When the sun set, the two said goodnight, agreeing to have breakfast together in the morning. They then both got into their own respective tents and went to sleep.

Sebastian arose with the sun and took Spike for a walk along the edge of the canyon. As the sun climbed over the horizon, he saw a lot of deer out foraging. Because there is no hunting in the national park, the deer weren't afraid of humans. Just the opposite, a few seemed almost to beg for food. Even the squirrels were aggressive and tried to steal food from people's hands. Hawks glided easily over the canyon, looking for their morning meal, along with an eagle or two.

When Sebastian got back to his tent, Rita was up waiting for him.

"Hi. Where have you been? Lady Luck has been looking for Spike."

"Nowhere special. Just checking out the area," answered Sebastian.

"Did you find a restaurant where we can eat?"

"Well, I did find a restaurant, but it's a little out of my price range."

"Don't worry about it. I make a decent salary and can afford to take my new friend out to breakfast. I can leave Lady Luck in the tent. Could Spike stay with her?"

"I don't see why not. It will probably keep her from whining the whole time you are gone," said Sebastian.

Rita and Sebastian were walking along the canyon path that followed the edge when Rita grabbed Sebastian's hand and squeezed.

"It's nice having a friend here," Rita said.

Sebastian was a little surprised by the show of affection but didn't mind. He wrapped his fingers around hers. Hand-in-hand, they approached the restaurant, which was a brown, log building. Upon entering, they were seated by a hostess wearing a tan National Park shirt. She was probably a college girl working the summer vacation. Their table was a simple mass-produced piece of furniture that probably was ordered for all the national parks in the nation. They sat next to each other on a bench long enough to accommodate four sets of buttocks. From their seats, they had a view of the canyon.

Rita ordered eggs, bacon, home fries, and toast. Sebastian had an order of flapjacks. They both had coffee. During breakfast, Sebastian began to inquire about her background.

"Have you always lived in Las Vegas?" asked Sebastian.

"Actually, I grew up outside of Phoenix, Arizona. I moved to Vegas after high school graduation. My parents wanted me to go to college, but I never cared for books too much. I like to be where the action is, and the action is in Las Vegas."

"Were your parents disappointed that you didn't continue in school?"

"A little at first, but they got over it. They realize that I'm responsible, hard working, and willing to follow my dreams."

"What are your dreams?" asked Sebastian.

"I want to be rich, live in a nice house, and, hopefully, be married with children."

"That sounds reasonable. I'm sure you will achieve your dream," replied Sebastian.

After a nice breakfast, they hurried back to the tent, not knowing what havoc the dogs may have wreaked. To their surprise, Spike and Lady Luck were both snuggled together sleeping in the tent. Never one to let sleeping dogs lie, Sebastian aroused them, getting them ready for a little exercise. He and Rita took the dogs for a long walk around the canyon edge. Sebastian was throwing the ball and Spike was retrieving it. Lady Luck was trying to imitate Spike, but wasn't living up to her name. Sebastian threw the ball a little too far, causing it to roll over the ledge. Spike stopped, but Lady Luck didn't and went over the edge after the ball.

Rita yelled. "Oh my God!" Tears began streaming down her face.

They ran to the edge and saw Lady Luck on a small piece of rock. She was about 15 feet below the ledge. There didn't look like any safe way to get down to rescue her. Lady Luck was starting to whimper, provoking a greater emotional response from Rita. Sebastian was trying to think of a way to retrieve her. He was afraid it would take too long to get a rope or help. Quickly scanning the area, Sebastian saw a path to the ledge too narrow for a person, but big enough for a dog. He told Spike to go get Lady Luck, pointing Spike in the right direction. Spike carefully did as he was asked. He gently walked along the ledge. Sebastian held his breath. As Spike walked, some small rocks went tumbling down the mountain hundreds of feet. When he finally reached Lady Luck, Spike grabbed the back of her neck in his mouth and slowly turned around. He then carefully walked the crevice until he neared the edge. Sebastian grabbed the dogs and pulled them up.

Rita was an emotional wreck at this point, her eyes bright red from the tears. She was still crying but also had a smile from ear to ear as she hugged her little puppy dog. Sebastian was proud of Spike. Once again, Spike had risen to the occasion and accomplished what had to be done without a lot of guidance. The four of them walked back to the campsite, this time with Lady Luck on a leash. Sebastian apologized for throwing the ball over the edge. Rita said no apologies were needed.

A few hours later, Rita told Sebastian that she had to get back to Las Vegas and asked if he would like a ride.

"Do they have any campgrounds there?" asked Sebastian.

"I don't know, but you and Spike are welcome to stay at my apartment. It's the least I can do for the dog that saved my puppy's life."

"Are you sure that wouldn't be inconveniencing you or your roommates?" asked Sebastian.

"Absolutely not. Besides, I don't have any roommates. I could give you a tour of Las Vegas and show you around the casino. Who knows, maybe you will get lucky at the slots or tables."

"I don't have any extra money to gamble, but I'd enjoy seeing Las Vegas."

The two got into the front seats of her Volkswagen, the dogs hopped in the back, and the camping gear was crammed into the front trunk. They were headed to Nevada.

Chapter 8

Sebastian, Rita, Spike, and Lady Luck arrived in Sin City that evening. After being in the Grand Canyon with its bare desert landscapes, the lights of Las Vegas were a little overwhelming to Sebastian. They pulled up to an apartment complex about a mile from the Flamingo Hotel.

"Is this where you live?" asked Sebastian.

"Yes, I've got a second-story apartment. Grab your gear and come on in."

"Wow, you've got a balcony overlooking the pool. This is really nice."

"Maybe we can take a swim later. Would you like that?" asked Rita.

"Sure," replied Sebastian.

"Let's take the dogs for a walk. Then I'll show you Las Vegas."

After getting their dogs straight, they hopped back into the Volkswagen and drove down the strip by the Sahara, Riviera, and down Fremont Street, where they parked. They then toured on foot. They stopped in Binion's and watched a little of the gambling.

"What do you think about these games? Do you like it?" asked Rita.

"I know how to play poker and blackjack, but I don't understand craps or any other European games like Baccarat. Besides, I've never had the free cash to spend on gambling," answered Sebastian.

"Don't worry. I'll see that you get to experience Las Vegas in more ways than one."

They stopped at a grocery store, picked up some fresh produce, milk, juice, dog food, and a few other items and went back to the apartment. Rita then opened up a bottle of Riunite red wine and poured two glasses.

"Get your bathing suit on, and we'll go for a swim," said Rita.

After a few glasses of wine, they were both feeling the effects of lowered inhibitions. Rita pushed Sebastian into the pool, and then followed him in, laughing all the while. Sebastian didn't have a muscular body, but rather a long, lean, fat-free physique. Rita's long blonde hair hung over the top part of her blue and yellow striped bikini. Sebastian surmised that she probably swam laps here quite often. Her swimsuit revealed a fit figure that glided across the pool with each stroke. After doing several laps of the breast, crawl, and the butterfly, Rita then swam underwater through Sebastian's legs, rubbing his crotch with the top of her head, surprising him as he sipped on his wine. She then came back and wrapped her legs around him as she hugged and caressed the side of his neck.

"That's just a sample of things to come," she said with a giggle.

"I'll take every sample you've got," replied Sebastian.

Noting that no one else was at the pool, Sebastian returned Rita's advances, and they spent the next hour in playful romance as they finished the bottle of wine.

"It's getting late. We better get to bed. I've got to work tomorrow afternoon."

"Where should I sleep?" asked Sebastian, a twinkle in his eye.

"Where else? With me."

With that remark, Sebastian grabbed her hand, leading her into the bedroom. They both started to remove each other's bathing suit. Rita pulled Sebastian into bed, pulling the covers up. She began to caress Sebastian on the side of his neck, while Sebastian moved his hands over her voluptuous breasts feeling the erect nipples with the tips of his fingers. As they assumed different positions, they continued their passions until they both reached a harmonious climax and then drifted off to sleep. The dogs must have sensed their symbiotic relationship, for they were sleeping curled up together at the foot of the bed.

"What's that horrible sound?" said Sebastian.

"That's my alarm clock. I like that sound because it is so annoying. It forces me to get out of bed to turn it off."

"What time do you have to be at work?"

"I've got to clock in no later than 2 p.m."

Rita sat back on the bed, resting her hand on Sebastian's chest. "It's twelve now, and I've got to set my hair, iron my uniform, feed and walk the dog, and get gas on the way to the Flamingo. By the way, you are coming with me to work. I told you last night, I want to show you the real Las Vegas."

Sebastian replied, "What am I supposed to do for eight hours while you work? I don't have much money, remember."

"You worry too much. I told you that I would take care of you. I will give you money to play with, but you'll have to play at someone else's table. If you play blackjack smart, like I tell you, or if you play roulette by red-black, or odd-even, you can stay there for a long time, without losing much money. Besides, you get free drinks while you play. You just have to tip the waitress. This will be good for you. Plus, when I get my breaks and dinner, we can be together. I'll have my friend the pit boss help you learn the other more difficult games. They sometimes have classes where they teach you how to play and when to bet."

Sebastian took Spike and Lady Luck for a walk while Rita prepared for work. After the dogs were properly cared for and fed, Rita and Sebastian went to a nearby restaurant for pizza. The restaurant was a throwback to old Italy, with images of gondolas, olive trees, and Mt. Etna on the walls. Soft Italian music was piped in through speakers in the corners. The owner had an Italian accent, dark complexion, ruddy cheeks, dark glasses, and thinning hair.

When Rita walked in, he yelled, "Hi, baby! I haven't seen you in a while. Where you been?"

"I've been here and there. Tony, this is my friend. His name is Sebastian."

Sebastian waved while Tony yelled, "You better take good care of my little girl. She is as sweet as candy."

Sebastian acknowledged the remark with a nod.

They ordered a twelve-inch pizza with mushrooms, green peppers, and onions. Rita sipped on a 7Up while Sebastian had a glass of water. During the lunch, Sebastian told Rita a little more of his background. They finished their pizza and headed to the casino.

Once a small town, Las Vegas was on the verge of becoming an urban destination for marriage, divorce, entertainment, and, of course, gambling. The "Rat Pack" had helped Las Vegas gain some of its notoriety. Frank Sinatra, Dean Martin, Sammy Davis, Jr., and Peter Lawford were a few of its group. They were popular entertainers who performed often at the Vegas clubs.

The casino at the Flamingo wasn't very crowded at this time of day, Rita explained, but would generate more business as the evening progressed. When they walked in, several people waved hello or hugged Rita. She seemed to be a popular employee. What got Sebastian's attention was the glitz of the casino. He had never been in a casino before, and he felt very much out of place.

"Sit over there, and I'll get you a beer. Then I have to check in and get my assignment."

Rita came back fifteen minutes later, gave Sebastian $25 in chips, grabbed his hand, and walked him over to the blackjack table. She told her friend Stephanie that Sebastian was her friend and to please help him with the basics of playing and betting. Stephanie assured Rita she would do her best, unless the table got crowded.

"Sebastian, I'll be right over there dealing stud poker. Stephanie will help you play. Madge will bring you free beers. I just can't be bothered while I'm dealing. If you get bored, take a break and go for a walk, or sit by the pool, okay?"

Sebastian began to get the knack of playing blackjack and soon had some luck playing. The table got more crowded, with all the seats taken by late afternoon. What bothered Sebastian the most was the cigarette smoke that permeated the room. The playing got more intense, and Sebastian felt himself getting sucked into the gambling feeling of having to win. He realized this could become a compulsion, as addictive as tobacco or alcohol.

He sat out for a while, relaxing and taking in the sights of the casino. He was watching a woman playing the slots when a man walked past and threw coins on the ground to the left of the lady. As she bent down to pick them up, another man came from the other side and grabbed her pocketbook. He began to walk for the door. Without thinking, Sebastian jumped up and tackled the man before he could reach the door. The commotion startled the room. Security came over, along with a host of onlookers. Sebastian gave his version of what had happened which was verified by the lady at the slot machine. Security handcuffed the man and hauled him away (probably to beat the crap out of him, Sebastian thought).

The hotel managers came to Sebastian and asked him to come to their office. The manager asked Sebastian a barrage of questions about his ideas and life history, which he answered very calmly. They offered him some food and beverages while they went to talk to the LVPD. After a short time, the managers came back and offered him a job doing security work in the casino on a temporary basis. A few of their employees had recently quit, and they needed somebody with a keen eye.

"With your appearance, nobody would suspect you as a security guard. But listen, we don't want you to confront the criminals, just notify the uniformed security guards," they told him.

Sebastian was shocked at the offer. At first, he brushed it off, but after some thought, he realized he could use some money. He didn't like being a mooch, letting Rita pay for everything, so he agreed to work for the next two weeks. He found Rita and told her about the job offer. She hugged and kissed him.

"Great! You and Spike can stay with Lady Luck and me."

"It's done. Then I can give you your $25 back, plus help with rent and food."

Rita shrugged. "Not necessary."

Sebastian went and filled out the necessary papers and spent the next five hours following a non-uniformed security man, getting pointers on what to look for in the casino. He learned various ways people cheat—ways that he never would have imagined. He realized his job was not just to catch card sharks, but also to prevent robberies of the type he had witnessed earlier.

"Hey, Sebastian. Rita told me about your journey and quest for enlightenment and all that bullshit. If you really want to find God, just lay down some cash, win, and line your pockets with good old Nevada greenbacks. By the way, my name is Chuck. I bartend at the Riviera, and this casino is my church. Remember, money makes the world go round, and the way to get it is to win big."

Chuck was a lean, tall guy with dark hair receding at the temple. He had an accent like he was from New York. He wore a dark gray disco suit with a blue collared shirt, the first two buttons open. His watch was gold, as were his onyx decorated cufflinks, and his shoes were black and pointed.

"I don't feel the same way as you, but it's nice to meet you."

"You don't think money makes life easier?" asked Chuck.

"That's not the point. Money and things will never make you truly happy and content. They can make you more comfortable, but without higher values, they just make a hollow shell around you. I also don't feel this is the best method of acquiring money, since casinos aren't built on the house losing."

"Maybe. But I'm gonna hit it big here one day. Then it will be easy street for me."

Rita got off work at 10 p.m., and Sebastian was waiting at the front door of the casino. They hurried home to let Spike and Lady Luck relieve their bladders. The dogs were happy to see them come home. They all went for a walk to a nearby park and then came back to the apartment.

"I saw you tackle that guy tonight. That impressed everybody at the casino. They don't usually offer a temporary position like you got. What kind of questions did management ask you?"

"They had me fill out a psychological personality profile, which I complied with. I'm not sure what they were looking for, but I must have fit the bill, 'cause they offered me that position."

"I'm just happy to have you around a while longer. Whatever the reason," said Rita.

The next day at the Flamingo, Sebastian was in covert mode, hanging around the casino, looking for bad guys. With his long hair and beard, wearing blue jeans, t-shirt, and work boots, Sebastian did not look like your typical security guard. Throughout the day, he mostly helped little ladies around the slot machines. He did help the other security guards confront an unruly drunk, and then he escorted him out of the casino. However, most of the day was boring and non-confrontational. By the end of the shift, he was getting a feel for the pulse of the casino.

That night, Rita and Sebastian went out with a few of Rita's friends to a local pub. In Las Vegas, Sebastian discovered, even the local pubs have slot machines. Her friends were a varied lot, having migrated to Vegas from all over the world. They had one thing in common: they liked a lively night life. Sebastian knew he couldn't carry on like this all the time. It was neither his style nor his intention, but it was an educating experience, and he did like Rita very much.

Sebastian sensed that Spike was starting to feel confined in Vegas. He couldn't stay outside while Sebastian worked at the casino, due to the leash law, heat, and lack of available space. Sebastian had given his word to the casino, and to Rita, so Spike would just have to endure the two weeks. Although Sebastian wasn't a traditional guy in appearance, he did have a strong personal ethic, and he always kept his word.

Sebastian managed to pass the time in the casino diligently, helping out whenever he could, but the glitz and glitter of Las Vegas was starting to irritate him. This environment, if he stayed in it too long, would have a damaging effect on his psyche. He thought a camping trip over the upcoming weekend would help. He and Rita could both work the day shift on Friday, leaving them time to travel after shift change. He approached Rita during her break, presented his plan to her, and waited for her input.

"Where would you like to go?" asked Rita.

"Someplace where there are trees and peace and quiet. I was actually thinking about visiting the Lake Tahoe area, up in the mountains. Have you ever been there?"

"No, but I've always wanted to go. It's a great idea. Lady Luck and Spike can run around without a leash, and I hear the weather there is much more pleasant in the summer."

The rest of the work week went well. Rita had the car packed on Thursday night, so at the end of their shift on Friday, they cashed their paychecks at the casino, picked up the dogs, and started their journey to the mountains of Nevada. Lake Tahoe sits on the Nevada-California border and is considered one of the largest lakes at high elevation in the world.

The Volkswagen Beetle managed to drive up the mountain flawlessly, but the trip was long. They didn't arrive until late that evening, immediately locating a campground that bordered the lake and had lots of trees. Sebastian signed them in and set up camp. The tent was going to be crowded with the two dogs inside. Once the campsite was established, they started a campfire within the designated spot. Rita had brought along some marshmallows, which they roasted on a stick. Spike even got a few, but Lady Luck wasn't interested. At the edge of the lake was a double swing. Rita and Sebastian hopped on and enjoyed the peaceful movement. The fresh air and the light of the moon were a nice change from the man-made surroundings of Las Vegas. After a while, all were tired, so they called it a night.

Morning came quickly. Once awake, getting out of the crowded tent was desirable. They found a hiking trail that started a few hundred yards from the campground and weaved into the mountains. They agreed this would be a good day for the trail. The temperature was in the 70s, and the air was crisp with a ten-mile-an-hour breeze. But first they finished their breakfast burritos, coffee, and juice, which came from the campground restaurant.

Spike led the way on the trail, with Lady Luck trying to keep up. Every so often Lady Luck would get distracted and chase a rabbit or squirrel into the woods. Rita would call her back and lecture her about leaving the trail. The vegetation was dense along the trail. Lots of firs, spruce, and rhododendron were among the flora that provided shade and cover. They walked a couple of miles before stopping for a snack, which comprised biscuits for the dogs and trail mix for the humans. While sitting there talking, they suddenly heard growling and then yelping nearby. Rita shrieked in fear. They looked in the woods and saw a fox nipping at Lady Luck's back. The yelping got louder. Sebastian jumped to his feet to chase the fox but then saw Spike pounce on it, tearing into its neck. The brutal attack from Spike forced the fox to abandon its prey and escape back into the woods. Rita immediately tended to Lady Luck. She noticed some bite marks but, luckily, nothing deeply penetrating. Rita was glad she had gotten Lady Luck her rabies shot. Spike was prancing around as if he was proud of himself. Needless to say Rita was impressed. Twice he had saved her little puppy.

Unfortunately, this ended the hike for the day. Rita carried Lady Luck back to the campground and applied an antibiotic to the wound. The rest of the weekend was spent around the campground, swimming, canoeing, fishing, and just enjoying the cooler mountain air, before heading back to Vegas.

On Monday, Lady Luck was healing well from her wound, and Sebastian and Rita were both back at work. This week they were working the 3-to-11 shift which gave them time to sleep in, swim in the mornings, take the dogs to the park, clean the apartment, and shop for anything they needed. After work, they still had time to go out to local bars and meet friends. Sebastian and Rita were getting along very well. The week was enjoyable with plenty of passion, fun, and, of course, some alcohol thrown into the mix. However, the bright lights of Las Vegas were wearing on Sebastian. He knew it was time to continue their journey. As much as he liked Rita, he knew he had to move on.

On Friday, Sebastian asked around the casino if anyone was driving west to the Los Angeles area. A man in his fifties with salt and pepper hair and a thick mustache said he would gladly take Sebastian and Spike. So, at shift's end, Sebastian said a reluctant goodbye to a teary-eyed Rita. They agreed to stay in touch, but she probably knew their brief affair was meant to be exactly that. The man, Stan Valentino, picked up Sebastian and Spike in a white 1968 Cadillac Eldorado and began driving west to L.A.

Chapter 9

The ride to L.A. began with not much talking. Then Stan began to tell Sebastian a little bit about his life. He worked for the Teamsters in the L.A. local union. He had started out with long-distance hauling but, later in his career, secured a position with the union, overseeing membership and organization.

Stan had grown up on the South Side of Chicago, but his family moved to the West Coast during the later years of the Great Depression. His dad had also driven a truck as his main occupation. Stan, although seemingly very open with his conversation, didn't appear to Sebastian to be very open-minded concerning people's lifestyles. He made a point of telling Sebastian that he didn't approve of his long hair, beard, and hippy lifestyle. The only reason that he was giving Sebastian a lift was that he visited the Flamingo often and was doing this as a favor to Rita.

"You know how to make a guy feel good," Sebastian said.

Stan was about 5 feet 10 inches tall, 210 pounds, and wore a black sport coat, gray slacks, and a gray collared shirt with black-and-gold cuff-links. He had a matching gray handkerchief stuck in the sport jacket's chest pocket. The top two buttons on his shirt were open, revealing salt and pepper chest hair. Attached to a small gold chain necklace hung a gold cross with a figure of Jesus on it. Stan's hair was long but well-groomed, slicked to the back.

During the ride, Stan chain-smoked, a Marlboro cigarette dangling from his mouth. He continually flicked the ashes out of the small, cracked-open vent window on the driver-side door. He must have had a severe case of acne as a youth, because his skin was pockmarked and rough. He had thick eyebrows, with a Roman nose, small lips, and yellow stained teeth.

He dominated the conversation. He turned his head right and looked in Sebastian's eyes and said, "I don't really need to hear your opinion on worldly things. What can a dumb-ass hippy with no money and no car teach me?"

Sebastian was just grateful to have a ride across the Mojave desert, so he kept quiet and listened to Stan's monologue.

Stan used the words "you know" incessantly. It was like those words were the proper grammatical end of a sentence. He was a big fan of Frank Sinatra and Jerry Vale, and he tried to locate them on different radio stations as he drove. Sebastian occasionally inquired into his job with the Teamsters, but Stan refused to get into specifics, letting Sebastian get the point that it was none of his f—kin' business. Sebastian quickly backed off.

The conversation got very heated when Stan started talking about his wife. Apparently, she had separated from him a little over a year earlier.

"Goddamn bitch. That f—kin' broad never had it so good. I treated her like a goddamn queen, you know. Who the hell does she think she is walking out on me after fifteen years of me paying her way? Why, it was never enough. Jewelry, luxury cars, nice clothing, wonderful vacations. What did I get in return? A note that says 'I need my space. My lawyer will be in touch with you. Good luck.'"

Sebastian listened intently, nodding to his points and letting Stan vent his anger and frustration. This was not a time that he wanted to give his opinions, or even to inquire into his wife's point of view.

After Stan started to calm down and talk about other subjects, the conversation drifted to Sebastian and why he was hitchhiking across the United States with a dog. This whole concept was entirely out of Stan's philosophical range. To Stan, life was practical: you worked to get money for nice vacations where you slept in a hotel bed, not on the ground in a sleeping bag.

"Let me get this straight. You are traveling around seeking 'enlightenment.' What the f—k is that all about? I mean, jeez, just go to your f—kin' priest, make confession, say a few Hail Mary's, and he'll tell you what to do. What more do you want, you know."

"Well, it goes a little beyond that. It's more like seeing the country and getting an idea of other people's thoughts, dreams, and realities. With the journey comes, hopefully, a life-changing situation, where I will grow spiritually as a person," said Sebastian.

"You want to grow spiritually, just f—kin' tithe at least ten percent of your income to the Church. That will get you on their big shot list. Who knows, maybe if you do it all your life, you'll get mentioned in Rome." Stan chuckled.

Sebastian just acknowledged his statement, knowing it was futile to discuss the point any longer. He changed the subject to where he could get dropped off. They were getting closer to Los Angeles, and he was anxious to reach the Pacific Ocean. Stan asked Sebastian where he was going. When Sebastian said near Manhattan Beach, Stan said that was good because he was heading right past there.

"Why are you going to Manhattan Beach?" asked Stan.

"I have an old Army buddy who lives out here. I hope to see him."

"Does he know your coming?"

"Not really. It was kind of an open invitation, whenever I could get out here," said Sebastian.

"I don't f—kin' believe it. First, that you, a goddamn hippy, was in the United States Army, and, second, that you think you can just show up on some guy's doorstep to stay anytime you feel like it."

"I'm afraid that's about the way it is," replied Sebastian.

"My God. Either I'm really getting old-fashioned or you're just f—kin' nuts, you know."

Sebastian didn't reply to that statement, preferring to let Stan wonder a little more about him.

"If you were in the U.S. Army, what was your unit?" asked Stan.

"I was in a military police detachment. I worked in a confinement facility."

"I don't believe it. A goddamn hippy in the military police, and a prison of all places. What was your job? Planting flowers in the prison?" Stan said with a disgusted look on his face.

"Actually, I started out in administration but ended up being a cell-block guard."

"Well, I'll bet you got a lot of 'enlightenment' there," Stan replied.

"Sometimes we can learn and grow in the most unpredictable places and times. Yes, it's true. We can learn from even the most downtrodden."

"Maybe for you, but no damn jailbird is gonna teach me nothing. If they are so smart, why did they get caught and land in jail? No. No jailbird is ever gonna be on my list of teachers," said Stan.

It was getting later in the evening. Sebastian appreciated the ride, but was getting tired of these conversations. Spike was quiet in the back seat, sleeping throughout the whole trip. They were beginning to see the lights of L.A. ahead. Sebastian had never been to the West Coast before and really had no idea where he was going. They had just arrived in L.A. when Stan said that he wanted to drive by his ex-wife's apartment before he would drop Sebastian off.

Sebastian didn't want to do this, but it was nighttime, and he didn't know his way around, so this was his only available option. They approached an upscale apartment house, and Stan started back raging about his wife leaving him.

"I'll tell you this. If I see any son-of-a-bitch go into her apartment, his tires are getting slashed," said Stan.

Stan pulled into a parking space and peered up at a window that had a light on. He kept repeating the phrase "I'll kill the son-of-a bitch." Needless to say, Sebastian was getting more uptight with each passing moment.

Stan pointed up to the window and said, "There she is, that f—kin' bitch. Why I oughta break her neck. It's just not right that she can get away with it. I'll tell you one thing, if I ever catch her screwing anybody else. . . ." He opened the glove compartment and lifted a silver revolver out and aimed it toward the window.

Sebastian was getting freaked out. He knew that this guy was totally capable of anything, and he just wanted to get out right then and there. He nicely asked if they could go soon, because it was getting late, and he didn't want to arrive at too ungodly an hour. Luckily, Stan was getting tired and agreed to go. Stan dropped Sebastian and Spike off a half-block from his destination. They said goodbye, and Sebastian was so relieved to be out of the car that he immediately threw his pack to the ground and picked up Spike, giving him a big kiss on his snoot.

"You were such a good dog in the car. Are you as overjoyed as I am to be back on terra firma?"

Chapter 10

Sebastian rapped on the door at 1736 Boise Lane. A middle-aged woman answered. She smiled but had an inquisitive look on her face.

"Is Randy home? My name is Sebastian, and this is Spike. I served with Randy in the U.S. Army overseas. We said we would get together, but this is my first time out to the West Coast."

"I'm afraid you picked a bad time. Randy went out of town and didn't tell me when he is coming back. I'm his mother. Why don't you come in for a cold drink? I'm sure Spike would like some fresh water."

"Okay," replied Sebastian.

They talked for a good hour, mostly about Sebastian and Randy's experiences in the Army. It was getting late, and they all needed some rest.

"Randy has his own apartment on the next block. I'll give you the key, and you and Spike can stay there until Randy gets back. Is that all right with you?"

"That would be just great. Thank you for your graciousness and trust," replied Sebastian.

Sebastian and Spike meandered down the block and found Randy's apartment. He unlocked the door, put down his pack, and flipped on the light switch. The room was small but neat. Posters of the Rolling Stones, Jimi Hendrix, and the Doors were in plastic frames hanging on the walls. Mother Earth magazine was laid out on the coffee table near some Zig Zag papers and a Mateus wine bottle with many colored drippings from old candles. An older sofa was behind the coffee table, and a matching tan chair with yellow pillows was on the other side of the room. Next to the chair was a long table with a nice turntable and receiver and the latest in Bose speakers. Underneath the table was a long row of albums, filed in alphabetical order.

Sebastian went into the kitchen and opened the refrigerator door, gratefully seeing a well-stocked supply of beer, some cheese and cold cuts, orange juice, and the usual condiments. The trip from Las Vegas had left him tired and thirsty. He quickly popped open a brew, flipped on a Judy Collins album, laid back, and enjoyed the moment. Sebastian felt they needed this personal time of peace and quiet to rest and regenerate before they continued their journey.

Spike picked up on Sebastian's contentment, went to the nearby bathroom, got himself a cold drink out of the toilet bowl, and then laid down by Sebastian.

"Spike, I think we are going to relax for a few days. Maybe we will go to the beach tomorrow," said Sebastian.

Spike wagged his tail, sensing he was included in the conversation. Eventually they both fell asleep.

Sebastian arose late the next morning and took Spike for a walk. On the way back, they stopped at a grocery store and picked up a few supplies, food, and a treat for Spike.

The beach was just under a mile away. The sun was bright, and Sebastian and Spike were ready for the Pacific Ocean. Sebastian wrote a note for Randy, just in case he came back while they were gone. They arrived at Manhattan Beach around noon. Sebastian threw the ball into the ocean, and Spike was happy to display his springer heritage, diving into the waves and quickly retrieving the ball. Again and again, Sebastian threw and Spike retrieved. Strangers stopped to watch and chat. Some teenagers invited him to a party that night, but Sebastian declined, not wanting to get mixed up in anything crazy at the moment.

Sebastian spent about four days at Randy's apartment, but Randy never showed up. During those days, Sebastian and Spike played at the beach and park. Sebastian read a book by Hermann Hesse called *Narcissus and Goldman.* He was starting to get bored and wanted to continue his trip. He once again went over to Randy's mom's house and rang the doorbell.

"Hello, Mrs. Chewning. We are going to leave since Randy never showed up. I just wanted to return his key and thank you very much for the hospitality." Sebastian held out some flowers he had picked in the park and wrapped in a sheet of newspaper. "I thought these would look nice in your vase."

"Why, Sebastian! How thoughtful of you. They are delightful. I shall enjoy them very much." She took the flowers. "I'm very sorry Randy never came home. He is like that sometimes. He gets on that Norton motorcycle that he brought home from the Army and just roams the West. It must be your whole generation. Seems everybody is always on the move."

Sebastian waved goodbye as he and Spike walked down the street. They were on their way to the beach again, but this time they were heading north with pack, tent, and sleeping bag. Sebastian didn't really have any idea of where he would stay, yet he didn't fear. He believed everything always works out.

They were playing on the beach, when they saw a young guy quietly freaking out. Sebastian asked if anything was the matter.

"Yes," he nearly yelled, a wild look in his eyes. "My grandfather gave me this watch, which has some very special memories, and I lost it in the sand somewhere around here. It's not the money that's important. But I distinctly remember him saying to me in his hospital room, 'I want you to keep this watch, and then pass it to your grandchild. It always brought me good luck.'"

"Maybe we can help."

"How can you help? I don't even know where to look."

"Give me an article of your clothing."

The young man handed him his sandals. Sebastian took them, called Spike over, and had him sniff the sandals. Sebastian then yelled, "Go find the watch."

Spike began to run around in a wide circle, tail wagging, nose to the ground. He was running between blankets, which some people weren't too happy about, but everyone was curious to see what this dog would do. Spike came back every few minutes and looked at Sebastian. Sebastian would point in another direction, and Spike would take off again, running in wide circles. After about twenty minutes, Spike came back with a gold watch in his mouth.

Sebastian laughed, pleased with Spike's success. The young man couldn't believe it. He was flabbergasted and very much relieved.

Spike was happy to have helped. The man then introduced himself as Jim. The only food he had were some dried papaya pieces, but he started feeding them to Spike while petting him on top of the head.

"I owe you guys big time. Now it's my turn to help you out. Where are you going? Can I give you a lift?"

"We are heading north. We don't have any real destination or schedule."

Jim shook his head. He really didn't know this concept, but he was cool with it.

"Come with me and I'll take you both where you want to go. My car is right off the beach. Grab your pack and follow me."

Jim led them to a white Austin-Healey sports car. He opened the door, said Spike could ride in the back, and directed Sebastian to put his pack on the luggage carrier on the trunk. The luggage rack had a couple of security cords with hooks to keep the pack from falling. The convertible top was down, so when they initially got in, the seats were a little hot on the tush. Off they went.

Jim liked to drive fast. As they drove through L.A. and the suburbs, Spike enjoyed the breeze in his face, and Sebastian was amazed at the luxuriousness of certain neighborhoods. Throughout the drive, Jim talked non-stop, often asking questions about Sebastian's personal history.

"So where are you from, and what the hell are you doing out here?"

After answering Jim's questions, Sebastian had one for him. "Where are you taking us?"

"First, I've got to stop at the jeweler and get this watch cleaned of all the sand that might have gotten in the mechanics. Then, I was going to stop at the In-and-Out burger joint for lunch."

"Great. We are enjoying the Southern California sights," replied Sebastian.

They were getting along great. But, as Jim came back from the jewelers, Sebastian made the mistake of saying "It must be nice to be born with a silver spoon."

Jim turned quickly and said, "Let's get one thing straight. I work for everything I get, so don't give me any shit."

Sebastian backed off, understanding that Jim was a little touchy about his possessions. They both quickly forgot about it.

As they pulled into the burger joint, Jim saw some buddies of his. They were standing by an older station wagon with three surfboards on the roof.

"Hey, dudes, what's up?" said Jim.

Several young guys surrounded the car, eyeing Sebastian and Spike.

"Who's your new pal?" said his taller friend, named Bo.

"Oh, this is Sebastian and his dog Spike. Spike saved my ass today, so I'm giving them a lift."

"Why don't you come to the party tonight. Bring Sebastian, too. It's gonna be wild. Almost every babe from Santa Monica is going to be there. Anybody can get laid there, even you, Jim," said Bo with a smile.

Jim turned to Sebastian and asked if he would like to go.

"That would be great, but what about my dog? Where can I leave him?"

"My dad has a small beach house in Malibu, on a cliff overlooking the Pacific. You can stay there for a while, and Spike can stay inside while we party," said Jim.

"You trust me to stay at your dad's house? That's really nice."

"Don't worry about it. There will be a collection agent looking you up one day," Jim joked. "You want anything inside?"

"No. At the present, I'm not eating any meat. But thanks anyway. I'll run across to the grocery store and pick up a few things."

They stayed awhile and then headed up the coastal highway toward Malibu.

"What do you do besides lose watches?" said Sebastian.

"I mostly pick up assholes with no car or money. Touché," laughed Jim. "I just graduated from UCLA and have been accepted into the UCLA medical school. I start in September."

"That's great. Do you know what kind of residency you will pursue?"

"I'm not sure, but I don't think it will be obstetrics/gynecology. I don't think I can trust myself. It would have to be awful tempting sometimes." He laughed. "Actually, I think that I may pursue surgery. Maybe even spine surgery. It takes a lot of talent and confidence—things that I don't lack. Besides, it probably pays very well, also. I'm very exact with my hands, which is needed in that field. What about you? Are you going to hitchhike your whole life?"

"I don't know what I want to do. I'm just trying find out about life and develop myself spiritually and philosophically before I actually settle into a career," said Sebastian.

"Spiritually? You mean like religion?"

"Yes. Religion and God or gods or high powers unnamed."

"Do you know anything about Judaism?"

"Not enough to give a lecture on it."

"Tomorrow night I am having a dinner at my parent's house, and my Uncle Morris will be there. He is a rabbi in the conservative synagogue. If you are interested, I'll ask my parents if you can come and get more enlightened."

"If it's not too much an inconvenience, I would be most happy to meet your family and learn the faith from one of knowledge. Please inform your parents ahead of time that I don't eat meat, so they don't think that I am being rude and impolite."

They drove up the coastal highway until they reached Malibu and pulled up to Jim's parent's beach house. It was a modest two-bedroom house sitting on a cliff overlooking the Pacific. The house was an off-white color with green shutters around the windows. The roof was a typical red tile. Approaching the house, they walked along a brick path leading to a doormat that said "Welcome to the Berlin Family Home." Sebastian was most impressed with the location and the ocean breeze.

"What a great place. Why don't your parents live here all year round?" asked Sebastian

"When you see their main residence, you'll understand. Besides, when you just come here occasionally, you appreciate it more."

They entered the house and viewed a very nicely furnished vacation home. The sofa and matching chairs were upscale, along with the tasteful coffee tables and lamps. The TV was one of Sony's newest. On one of the walls overlooking the stairs, Sebastian could see pictures of Jim and his sisters dressed in prayer shawls and yarmulke.

"Those are pictures from our Bar and Bat Mitzvahs," Jim said. "Big events. They represent the achievement of becoming a man or woman."

Sebastian nodded.

"Are you sure your parents won't mind Spike and me staying here?" asked Sebastian.

"My parents have always taught me to help someone in need. As long as you take care of the place, it will be all right. Even though you look like shit, my gut feeling tells me you are honest and good for your word. Besides, I'm doing this for Spike."

"Don't worry about Spike. He won't chew any furniture. He will just hang out where I tell him to."

"Well, Mr. Vegetarian Man, what do you do for fun? I mean, you're not queer or anything, are you?"

"Even though I'm on a quest, I like to have a good time as much as the next, as long as the fun is not at anybody's expense. In answer to your question, I am very much of a heterosexual temperament," replied Sebastian.

They continued through the house, and Jim showed him to the guest bedroom. It was a cozy room, with red and blue décor—blue walls with red accented artwork hanging in red frames. The bedspread was blue with red pillows. A Tiffany lamp hung over a small table in the far corner of the room. From the table, you could see the ocean waves banging against the rocks to the north. A few family photos sat perched on the cherry wood bureau. One was a picture of Jim, about four years old, sitting in a toy Ferrari automobile. His smile was from ear to ear.

"Let's go to Venice Beach before we go to the party. It's a great place to see a wide assortment of people. By the way, you don't use drugs, do you? I'd rather you didn't while you are staying here."

"Don't worry, Jim. I respect your wishes. I'm not into that on this trip."

Walking along Venice Beach was quite a sight. It had something for everybody—everything from bodybuilders, chess players, artists, druggies, volleyball games, and the usual assortment of food and gift shops skirted the beach.

After spending some time there, Jim turned to Sebastian and said, "How would you like to meet some really hot babes?"

"What do you think? But can they enlighten me?"

"We are not talking at a high level now," said Jim.

"What about that party we were invited to?" said Sebastian.

"We can go later. I have a good friend who can get us in to the

Playboy Mansion. They are having a poolside gathering this evening. It's a tribute to the UCLA Medical School. Some of the attending physicians perform aesthetic surgery on many of the playmates. As thanks for all their wonderful care, they have a bash once a year. Needless to say, not too many doctors want to turn this party down. Are you up for this?"

"Who wouldn't be?" replied Sebastian.

Jim lent Sebastian a decent collared shirt and Bermuda shorts so he would be more presentable. Jim was always upscale. Whether it be clothes, cars, or personal equipment, he had to have the best. They arrived at the mansion a little after 7 p.m. They had little trouble getting in. Jim had secured an invitation earlier that week. They were escorted to poolside. As they gazed around, Sebastian thought he may be in paradise. There must have been thirty Playmates in bikinis lounging and socializing around the pool. Waiters came around with hors d'oeuvres, mixed drinks, and almost any fruit imaginable.

Although Jim and Sebastian were considerably younger than many of the other men there, several Playmates came by and introduced themselves and wished them a nice time. Jim was a very verbal, outgoing guy, whereas Sebastian was a little more introverted. Jim was doing all the talking and never missed a beat. Some of the Playmates enjoyed his witty remarks and conversation.

"Are you enjoying this party?" Jim asked Sebastian.

Surrounded by a few Playmates that were interested in Sebastian's journey, he turned and whispered to Jim, "I think my thoughts aren't so spiritual tonight."

The party lasted a few hours. Jim tried to get phone numbers, but the Playmates were under pretty strict watch and were asked to keep their contacts to a minimum while staying at the mansion. However, one of the more intriguing Bunnies slipped Jim a paper with her home phone and address, asking him to give her a call at the end of the year. The evening was like a fantasy, but all fantasies end. They said goodnight to many and got back in the Austin Healey.

Leaving the mansion, they drove through Beverly Hills, eyeing one fantastic estate after another. Jim pointed out the homes of various Hollywood celebrities. He showed Sebastian Charlie Chaplin's old house and then drove past Elizabeth Taylor's home.

The party afterward was a bust, so Jim dropped Sebastian off in Malibu and went home. Spike was happy to see Sebastian come home and ready to go for a walk. The breeze was refreshing, so they sat outside for a couple of hours, enjoying the California coast.

The next day, Jim picked Sebastian up and headed to the beach. Jim had a couple of surfboards sticking out of the back of his car. Having never surfed before, Sebastian had a little difficulty getting up. However, when he put Spike on the board with Sebastian sitting, they both rode a wave in. Spike enjoyed hanging ten in the ocean. Jim had little trouble getting up, but he couldn't stay up very long. After they all had a fun day at the beach, Jim took them to Trader Joe's to pick up some food. He said he would see Sebastian later for dinner that night, when Sebastian was to meet Jim's uncle.

As they walked into the house, Jim's parents didn't quite understand the connection. Jim wore the latest golf-style shirt with well-pressed khakis and another fancy diamond-laden watch on his left wrist, along with cordovan penny loafers. This with Sebastian, the laid-back, bearded vagabond. Whatever Jim's parent's thought, they were perfectly gracious and hospitable. Mrs. Berlin served homemade chicken soup as an appetizer, with Chilean sea bass, asparagus, and baked potatoes for the main course. Ending the meal was a delicious blueberry cheesecake and Columbian coffee for dessert.

During the meal, the conversation focused mostly on family affairs. Sebastian stayed quiet and listened. However, he noticed Jim's Uncle Morris gazing at him throughout. The family moved to the living room after the meal, but Jim's uncle motioned for Sebastian to come out on the porch. Sebastian followed and saw that the rabbi motioned for him to sit down, which he did.

"Jim tells me that you are interested in learning about Judaism. Is that true?"

"Well, it's not just Judaism. I would like to learn about a lot of different faiths."

"I don't know about the rest, but if you are willing, I can inform you about Judaism. What would you like to know?" said the rabbi.

"What is the essence of Judaism?" asked Sebastian.

The rabbi smiled. "You get right to the point. Judaism is a very complicated mixture of schools of thought and sects. However, one very dominant theme is the idea of a monotheistic, all-knowing God that cannot be worshipped with pagan idols. Plus, the scrolls of the Torah are the basis for all Jewish learning."

"Is that all there is?"

"Absolutely not. We could sit here for days and still not cover all the aspects, but to sum up: to follow the faith one must enter into a covenant with God, and in doing so must live their life according to the virtues and values that come with acceptance of His commandments. The idea of family is very important. It is considered man's responsibility to marry and father children. Another responsibility is continued learning and education. A third is the responsibility to the Jewish community."

Sebastian and the rabbi talked for a good while. Sebastian asked questions, and the rabbi tried to answer them as best he could in terms that Sebastian would understand. Finally, Jim came in and said that they had to leave. Sebastian thanked the rabbi for the conversation and enlightenment. He then thanked Jim's parents for the meal and the hospitality at their vacation home.

Jim and Sebastian spent the last evening out visiting Santa Barbara, Rodeo Drive, and a few other spots. Jim told Sebastian that he would not be available the next day. Sebastian got the hint and said that he and Spike would be on their way.

The next morning, Jim picked Sebastian and Spike up and took them to the PCH (Pacific Coastal Highway). They both felt like they had made a lasting friendship. Sebastian wished Jim the best in medical school. Jim waved goodbye and drove off.

Chapter 11

Sebastian and Spike sat along the coastal highway, enjoying the sun and breeze, when a new white Lincoln Continental stopped. A well-dressed man in his fifties, balding on top with gray on the sides, rolled down his window and asked him if he wanted a ride. Sebastian replied yes. The man opened the trunk and signaled Sebastian to put his pack in, which he did. The man then laid a large blanket over the seat so Spike wouldn't soil the covers. He introduced himself as John Abernathy from San Luis Obispo. Spike got in the back, and Sebastian the front.

"I can take you as far as San Luis Obispo. Is that all right?"

"That's perfect. We appreciate any hospitality. Thank you," replied Sebastian.

Sebastian watched John, who was wearing a gray pinstripe suit with engraved initials on the breast pocket, a white button-down long-sleeve shirt with cuff links, and a gray and black necktie with gold dollar signs scattered on it. His black loafers were well shined, as were his manicured nails. On his fingers were a couple of expensive gold and diamond rings, one with a square and compass, a symbol of the Masons. The other ring had an image of a skyscraper.

"Excuse me, sir. We are surprised that you stopped and picked us up."

"Why is that?" asked John.

"Well, you are so well dressed and classy. You're not our usual type of ride," replied Sebastian.

"As a matter of fact, I don't usually pick up hitchhikers. But you reminded me of my son, whom I haven't heard from in a while. Your dog and you didn't appear to be a threat."

"I like that, because I don't want to appear threatening to anybody. Neither does Spike," replied Sebastian.

"The last I heard from my son, he was leaving to live in a commune in Tennessee and 'get back to the land.' I personally don't understand it. He is educated, has everything he could want, yet he says the material world is not for him. I was hopeful that he would one day lead my corporation. But no. He said he was on a journey to know God. Are you on that same trip?" asked Mr. Abernathy.

"Sort of, but I'm more of a loner than a group personality."

They were cruising down the coastal highway where the beauty is unbelievable, with winding curves and breathtaking vistas around every turn. Sebastian listened to John while trying to enjoy the California beauty.

"I don't get it, Sebastian. What's wrong with living luxuriously? Having money is wonderful. It gives one freedom to accomplish what you want to and the means to not worry about having the necessary funds to meet your goals. Money is God in our society, whether you hippies like it or not. America was built on investments. Money and spirituality are not antithesis to each other. One can have both. In fact, one helps the other. Yet my son and many others are spurning the material world for this communal life. I just don't get it," Mr. Abernathy said while throwing his hands up in disgust.

"I'm not disagreeing with you, sir, but every generation has to go through their own process of self-discovery. Maybe the material life doesn't mean as much if it's handed to them without self-achievement," said Sebastian.

"You have a point, but then go out and work and study to achieve your goals, not join some commune. America is great because of its rugged individualism, not some bunch of Reds telling everybody how to think, what to do, and what you can and can't have. My goodness. It's the accumulation of wealth that lets charities flourish in our country. Without corporate wealth, ninety percent of your charitable contributions would dry up."

Mr. Abernathy continued to expound on the righteousness of capitalism and Christianity. Sebastian listened to examples of the people who have achieved the American dream, thanks to the American capitalistic ideal. Sebastian didn't get a chance to talk, yet he was interested in the conversation. Mr. Abernathy had a valid viewpoint that was every much as worthy of consideration as anything else.

"What interests you, Sebastian?"

"Many things at the moment, but most of all people interest me. I'm fascinated with man and the institutions that are created through him. I guess I have a little social scientist, politician, and clergyman inside me," replied Sebastian.

"That sounds like a dangerous trinity. What you need is to get your hands dirty and do some hard work. That will get you on the right track. Instead of trying to cure the world of its ills—which you will never do—just accomplish a few things that matter in the here and now," said Mr. Abernathy.

"If I'm not too brash, what do you do for a living?" asked Sebastian.

"I'm a builder and developer. Yes, I worked my way up through the ranks, saved money, got a few lucky breaks, and wasn't afraid to take a few chances, or get my hands dirty."

"What kind of building do you do?"

"All commercial. Nothing residential. I've always had large, grandiose ideas, and I was willing to work to achieve them. I must say, I've been pretty successful."

"That ring on your finger, does that mean you are a Freemason? And what does a Freemason do?"

"I am a member of the Masonic Lodge, and that's all I'm willing to discuss right now."

Sebastian took notice. He had heard that Freemasons were something of a secret organization dating back centuries and that members were forbidden to discuss it with non-members. He wondered how they got new members if they couldn't talk about it.

"Where are you going to on your trip?" asked John.

"Wherever the journey takes me. I have nothing set in stone. That way I'm open to many possibilities, should they present themselves."

"What do your parents think about your journey?"

"It doesn't matter. I'm not a child. I make my own decisions. I don't ask them for anything. Of course, I keep in touch, whether I'm traveling or not."

"How do you support yourself?"

"I've been working in the service industry, mostly food and beverage. But I have done many types of work. To go on this journey, I saved some money and, if need be, I will work along the way. If one is not too proud, work can always be found."

"I do appreciate your work ethic. There's too many welfare recipients in our society. They are like parasites, sucking income from the hard-working people."

The Lincoln motored comfortably up the California coast as Sebastian took a short nap. They passed Santa Barbara, Carpenteria, and other Spanish-sounding names. When Sebastian awoke, he saw a road sign that said San Luiz Obispo, 20 miles ahead. He quickly sat up knowing that the ride would be ending shortly. Looking at the map, he decided that he would spend the night at Morro Bay. There was a state park, and it was on the beach. That was always a good combination.

Arriving in San Luis Obispo, Mr. Abernathy drove some distance out of his way to take Sebastian and Spike to Morro Bay. After helping them with their pack, Mr. Abernathy wished them luck, shook Sebastian's hand, and went south toward his home.

Chapter 12

Spike and Sebastian spent the rest of the day and night at Morro Bay State Park and beach. It was a beautiful place. The ocean was fantastic and the scenery idyllic. After waiting for the office to close, Sebastian found a nice tree-covered flat piece of grass to set up his tent. He didn't have a car, nor need a campfire site, so he didn't feel like he was using up anybody else's space. He just used the cold showers, toilets, and water fountains. After a tiring day, they both slept very quickly.

The next day, Spike and Sebastian were back on Route 1 when a huge bus stopped. Scripted letters on the side read "Subconscious Invasion." The door swung open, and the driver motioned for them to get in the bus. Hesitantly, Sebastian and Spike maneuvered into the bus and looked around. It was custom made. Most of the seats had been removed, and comfortable chairs, tables, and beds took their place. At the far end was a small kitchen and a place for musical instruments. Curtains gracefully skirted the windows.

Seated around a table were five long-haired men in their twenties and an attractive girl about the same age. Seated up by the bus driver was an older man, appearing to be in his forties. A cute little beagle ran up and started smelling Spike's rear end.

"He's the reason we stopped," said one fellow, who introduced himself as Greg. "I thought my dog could use some company. Anyway, welcome to our home on the road. We are Subconscious Invasion. You ever hear of us?"

Sebastian wasn't sure but, tactfully, he acknowledged that although he had never seen them, he knew of people who had.

"This is John on drums, Mike on bass, Austin on piano and

keyboard, Phil on flute and many other instruments, myself on lead guitar, and last but not least, our lead singer and the glue that keeps us together, Angela."

They all said hello and tried to make him feel comfortable. Spike was already in the back with Ernie the beagle. Sebastian thought this was a pretty cool ride; they all seemed pretty nice.

"Where are you going?" asked Greg.

"Nowhere special," replied Sebastian.

"As long as you're not a pain in the ass, you can hang with us for a while. We have a gig at The Fillmore tomorrow night. We are the opening band for the Allman Brothers. Here, get yourself comfortable."

Greg, who appeared to be the alpha male of the pack, handed Sebastian a cold Michelob. As they rode up the coast, some were tuning their instruments, others looking out the windows or reading. The older fellow up front, Sebastian surmised, had to be their business manager.

"How did you acquire your band's name?" asked Sebastian.

"We like our music to leave a lasting impression," said Greg.

As Sebastian was drinking his beer, Angela came over and started talking to him. She was very friendly. Sebastian kind of sensed that Angela was used to getting what she wanted. Thoughts raced through his mind. He didn't know the relationship between Angela and the rest of the band, and he didn't want to upset anyone. Also, he knew that many bands used illegal substances. Maybe she was checking him out to be sure he wasn't a narc. In the end, Sebastian would just have to play each moment by ear and just be himself.

"Do you play any music yourself?" asked Austin.

"No. Wish I did. I just play my own little blues harmonica, making up tunes as I go along. I can't read music or anything like that," replied Sebastian.

"That's cool. Maybe one time you could join in a jam here in the bus, when we are just goofing around."

Sebastian just smiled, knowing he couldn't hold a candle to these guys.

Meanwhile, the bus continued its trek up the California coastline, stopping for lunch at Big Sur. They piled out and headed for a restaurant that overlooked the breaking waves of the Pacific

Ocean. Sebastian wasn't sure what to do. The restaurant looked fancy, and he didn't have the money to spend at fancy restaurants.

As he hesitated, the older man from the bus came over and casually said, "I know you don't have much cash, so as long as you are the guest of the band, your expenses will be paid and considered a business write-off. We will consider you a roadie. Okay?"

Sebastian thanked him with a handshake and a warm smile.

The restaurant was beautifully decorated with a unique color design. The walkway to the restaurant featured long rows of purple, white, and pink flowers. The flowers in the window boxes hanging on each ledge matched those on the path. Inside, glass windows let the sunshine light the room, giving it the feeling of outdoors. In front of each window hung a plant from the ceiling. Each table had a bright-colored tablecloth over it and a colored candle on a ceramic plate. The furniture was all hand-built, not run-of-the-mill factory-made. Each chair had a comfortable matching-color seat cushion.

The group was led through the room and out onto a patio that overlooked the ocean. A stone wall surrounded the patio, preventing anyone from accidentally going over the edge. The wall had tiles on its top with torches every six feet to give it light in the evening. Evidently, the band had made reservations, because a long table was already set for the group. Chilled wine was in ice buckets by the table. Sebastian was impressed.

"Don't be shy. Order what you like, Sebastian," said the business manager, Steve. The meal was wonderful. While most of the band ordered steaks or seafood, Sebastian just ordered a Southwestern-style rice, beans, and cheese dish with a side salad. By the end of the meal, the band was feeling pretty good. They managed to deplete several bottles of wine. Back in the bus, everybody was very comfortable, and one of the members brought out a pipe with blonde hashish and started passing it around. Not all members accepted it, including Greg, which made Sebastian feel good. He didn't want to be odd man out. After that, many members drifted off to sleep.

"I noticed you didn't take a toke on the pipe," Greg said to Sebastian.

"No, I'm looking for other ways to take me higher," replied Sebastian.

"That's good. Even though I occasionally hit it, I prefer a less clouded head. What are you doing out here on the road? I mean traveling 3,000 miles from your home with a dog and hardly any money?" said Greg.

Sebastian looked around the bus. "This is exactly what I'm looking for. I mean, if I stayed home, I certainly wouldn't be going to a concert with Subconscious Invasion and the Allman Brothers, would I?"

"I suppose you are right, but I would imagine all your rides aren't like this."

"Absolutely. But one can learn from all situations, good and bad. Of course, we always hope for the good," said Sebastian.

"Even so, I certainly couldn't do what you are doing, nor do I want to," said Greg.

Dusk was approaching when the beautiful scenic coastal highway gave way to larger and uglier interstate systems. The traffic was becoming more congested as they approached San Francisco. The bus continued through the city and stopped at a large hotel down the street from The Fillmore. As they unloaded, Sebastian offered to help with the instruments. They said there was no need because a van full of roadies was already unloading at the concert site. The band was responsible only for their own personal belongings. Very nice, Sebastian thought.

"You don't mind sleeping on the couch in the suite do you, Sebastian?" said Steve.

"Oh, no. I'm grateful for any sleeping arrangements you have, as long as my dog can stay there."

"As long as he is quiet. We usually sneak Ernie up later on. Tonight, we are all going down to The Fillmore to test out the acoustics and get a feel for the hall. We have got a wild concert tomorrow night. There is supposed to be a solo singer and guitarist early in the evening, before we get on the stage, and of course we precede the Allman Brothers."

Later, down at The Fillmore, Sebastian thought it was an awesome feeling, being in the hall where some of the best musical acts of the '60s had performed. Sebastian just sat there and imagined Janis Joplin singing "Ball and Chain" or Jimmy Hendrix performing "Foxy Lady." Subconscious Invasion tested out their instruments and performed some of their music. They were very good. Their music was an eclectic mix of styles, leaving the listener unable to place them in a category. Sebastian especially liked their songs "Psychodyllic Rhapsody" and "Imaginary Misconception." They wrapped up their session and went back to the hotel. When they got back, boxes of fresh pizza were waiting, along with ice cold beer. The evening ended on a high note.

The next day as the band was getting ready for the concert, Sebastian could sense a little nervousness permeating the group. Each member dealt with nerves in a different way. Some lit up cannabis sativa, others drank alcohol, and Steve, their manager, he put on his running shoes and shorts and went for a run in San Francisco. They all realized that they would be under the spotlight that night and didn't want to mess up. A good performance at The Fillmore could open up many doors and maybe lead to a recording contract.

Angela was the most relaxed of the group. She was also the most animated of the group, tickling people, singing to them, trying to get everybody up for the concert.

Although they didn't try to match their clothes for the concert, they did try to coordinate colors. Sebastian tried to help with whatever was needed, since they were being so nice to him. He ran out for coffee and doughnuts in the morning and later helped set up the stage. But most of all, it was Sebastian's calming influence that somehow helped relax the group.

There were quite a few groupies hanging around the hotel. Although many would have liked to party with the Invasion, most were really looking for the headlining band. Groupies were good for young bands' egos and often helped their sex lives out, but for the more mature artists, they were just silly, annoying youth.

Later in the day, the group ate dinner, got dressed in the hotel, and prepared for The Fillmore. They were supposed to go on around 8 p.m. and the Allman Brothers about 9. The solo guitarist was to kick things off at 7:30. They arrived at The Fillmore about 7:20. The place was starting to fill up. As they were tuning up in the back, they realized that it was 7:40 and no one was performing yet. The stage manager went back to the changing room and found the soloist totally stoned. He was out of it, like he had taken downers with alcohol. The crowd was waiting for some entertainment. The group wasn't ready to perform just yet, and everybody was in a quandary over what to do.

Sebastian cleared his throat and said, "I can keep them entertained for a little while. Just give me a few minutes."

He ran out to the bus, grabbed Spike and a blues harmonica, and ran back in. The group looked confused.

Sebastian went on stage, grabbed the microphone and said, "What's up, people?" Not getting much response, he said, "You've heard of greyhounds, and you've heard of bloodhounds. Well, this is Spike, the baddest blues hound of them all."

The crowd started shouting, "Spike! Spike!"

Sebastian got out his blues harp and started playing a soulful blues tune, and Spike started to howl in tune with the harmonica. When Sebastian hit a higher note, Spike stuck his snoot straight up and hit the high sounds. Then, when Sebastian took it low and slow, Spike brought his snoot lower and dragged out some low sounding howls. The audience was loving it. They started to clap, hoot, and holler. When Sebastian finished that tune, the crowd yelled for more. They had a few more minutes, so Sebastian and Spike did a houndful rendition of "Summertime," which was enjoyed immensely by the whole place. When they came off the stage, everybody was petting Spike and slapping Sebastian on the shoulder.

Once the amusement was over, Subconscious Invasion had to regroup and get serious, for they were about to go on stage. The emcee came out and introduced them as the hottest up-and-coming band on the West Coast, a band that writes all their own music, Subconscious Invasion.

They all walked out and assumed their instruments, while Angela, the thin and tall, long-blonde-haired lead singer grabbed the microphone and shouted, "Kick back and be ready to rock!"

They started off with a rockin' number called "Bustin' out the Faith," which Greg had written years earlier. His stepfather had told him that he would never amount to anything, so one night, he had written this song about the faith he had in himself, a faith that nobody could destroy. The next song, "Modified Behavior," was about Angela's teenage years. Her parents hadn't liked her choice of lifestyle, so they made her see a psychotherapist who said she needed to modify her behavior.

The band had the audience enthralled. With each new song, the noise got positively more vibrant and vocal. The Invasion followed with "Fever in my Soul," a tune written by Angela about the fire within her, driving her to seek her destiny. This led into the rocking favorite "Keep the Fire Burning," a tune written by Austin, about why their generation must continue the quest to take this world to a new level. They broke out into a jam during the middle of the tune. It was almost 9:10 when the Invasion got the crowd ready for the Allman Brothers by playing "Psychodyllic Rhapsody." This tune, with its long guitar solo, got the house rockin', so when they finished, the crowd was chanting for its headline act.

Subconscious Invasion were pleased with their performance. They sat back and enjoyed the Allman Brothers' show along with the audience. The Allman Brothers' performance lasted two and half hours and had the audience on their feet the whole time. Throughout the evening, the odor of hemp and hash saturated the room. Blurry eyed freaks wandered out of The Fillmore with shit-eating grins across their faces.

After the show, back at the hotel suites of both bands, a party was roaring. Sebastian was enjoying a beer when one of the stars approached, shook his hand, and said, "Thanks for helping out the concert. That was just great."

Sebastian was plain dumbfounded that one of the legends of rock would say that to him. Spike was making his rounds, getting party snacks from everyone he could mooch off. There were many attractive young females circulating through the party, hoping to spend the night with a band member. Some achieved their goal. Sebastian, however, had a little too much alcohol and drifted off to sleep alone.

He awoke late the next morning to Spike whimpering to go outside. Sebastian took him out. The band was getting ready to pack up and head to their next gig at the University of Nebraska. Sebastian and Spike were staying in California, so Sebastian helped the band pack, shook hands with all, and hugged Angela goodbye. However, as Steve was boarding the bus, he handed Sebastian an envelope from The Fillmore. Inside was three hundred dollars, payment for performing the first act of the night. Sebastian just smiled and thanked him for everything.

Chapter 13

Sebastian and Spike wandered around the streets of San Francisco. The town was a hotbed of liberal ideas, psychedelic happenings, and varied outlooks on life. Sebastian generally didn't like staying in large cities, not only because of the traffic and violence, but also for Spike's well being. It was difficult to be in a city with a dog who hardly ever had a leash attached. There were few public grassy areas and little room for Spike to relieve himself. Sebastian also felt some of the constraints of the crowded city. However, one of the main problems was finding a decent place to sleep with very little money. Luckily, Sebastian believed that things always work out.

Sebastian and Spike were walking down a tree-shaded street, when a van stopped. Inside sat a man and woman in their mid-twenties. The man was wearing khaki pants, a blue button-down short-sleeved shirt, and tennis shoes. His blonde hair was cut short and neat. The woman had long dirty-blonde hair. She wore a white summer dress with sandals.

"Where are you going?" she asked.

Sebastian replied, "We don't really have a destination."

The man and woman looked at each other, smiling. "You can come with us."

Sebastian didn't think these people were violent, so he nodded and he and Spike got into the back of the white work van.

Sitting in the second row of the van, Sebastian noticed flowers in buckets of water throughout the van. He also noticed a picture of an Oriental man on the dashboard of the van.

"What are the flowers for?"

"We sell flowers at the San Francisco airport, and the proceeds go to our church."

Sebastian thought that was a very nice gesture, with a good work ethic. The woman began asking about Sebastian's life—what was his religious foundation, was he happy and content with his spiritual life? Of course, Sebastian always enjoyed a good healthy conversation about spiritual development. During the talk, Sebastian sensed that these people were not just being nice, but that they had some kind of agenda. What it was, he did not know.

The van careened onto the expressway and headed for another part of town. Sebastian was tired and hoped that these people could provide a place to stay for the night. It was getting very late in the day, and this was a chore that had to be done. As the van sped down a boulevard, Sebastian asked about the Oriental man on the dashboard.

"He is our supreme master, Reverend Sun Yung Sun, the head of our Church."

The words "supreme master" were two words that made Sebastian cringe inside. Never one to follow blindly, he would have asked to leave then, but he was interested in researching their faith further. After another five-minute ride, the van pulled into the driveway of a large white building that looked like a dormitory, temple, and office all in one. They all got out of the van, and Sebastian offered to help them carry the flowers to the building.

At the door, they took off their shoes and motioned for Sebastian to do the same, which he did. Then, when Sebastian opened the door for Spike, they said that Spike could not come inside. Sebastian was annoyed. They knew he was traveling with his dog, and he felt this was a little sneaky. They should have told him before. Sebastian told Spike to wait outside and gave him some dog food and water.

Once inside, Sebastian was greeted by what appeared to be people of similar stature who must have belonged to this church. They had also brought in a haggard band of misfits, Sebastian included. Sebastian remembered reading a book called *The True Believer,* by Eric Hoffer, in which the author pointed out that people ripe for the picking were these true believers. They usually were younger, lonely, and looking for belonging. They were hitchhikers waiting for the ride of their life. Sebastian felt that he was seeing this play out in front of him.

Hors d'oeuvres were passed around, and a few prayers were said. Then the pitch began. A man preached that the better life could be found. "Just follow the guidance of Reverend Sun Yung Sun. You can all find the love of God. Just come out to the retreat in Mendocino County, just north of the city. By seeking the Master, through guidance, prayers, and hard work, you will find your way. We all work for the Supreme Master, for he is the light that leads our way."

Sebastian was very skeptical, especially when he was asked for a hefty donation for his weekend stay at the retreat.

What kind of retreat was this? he thought. Paying to work.

But, Sebastian was still interested in going. He wanted to observe this organization, and having a place in the country to stay would be an added benefit. He asked to see the person in charge. He stated his case, explaining that he had very little money but was willing to work, as long as he could bring his dog, Spike.

The leader reluctantly agreed, mostly because having a new convert was more important than gaining monetarily.

The gathering lasted a few hours, with the converts interviewing their new prospects incessantly. When someone appeared to be too strong willed or not open to converting, he or she was asked to leave the building immediately. Of course, this was done tactfully, so as not to draw attention to any defiance. As the gathering ended, Sebastian set up a tent in the backyard and slept with Spike at his side.

Morning came early, and the devotees hurried everyone to the waiting vans. They had a total passenger list of twenty-four: eighteen recruits and six devotees. What a group of people. Some were young and idealistic; others were just searching for something to believe in since they had no sense of self. There were one or two who truly believed in the mission of Reverend Sun Yung Sun.

The ride was pleasant as they got a view of San Francisco, the Golden Gate Bridge, and the California countryside. Spike liked hanging his head out the window, with his ears horizontal in the breeze. The two vans slowed down about two hours later.

As the van approached the church property, there were a lot of people with signs. A sheriff's car was there as well, along with a group of news reporters. As they made their way through the people, Sebastian got a closer look at the signs. One read "Sun Yung Sun's church is a cult and they brainwash young kids." Another said "Give my son back." The reporters were interviewing the parents and protesters outside the church property. Evidently, many parents had adult children who were breaking away from their families and not keeping in touch. The church would not let visitors onto the property, and the devotees were not coming out.

Sebastian thought about how organizations like this want total control over their members, physically, mentally, and spiritually.

The driver got out, unlocked the gate, and drove into the compound. Sebastian noticed fields of corn, wheat, vegetables, and grapes along the dirt road. The van pulled up to a compound with numerous buildings. Sebastian surmised that these were sleeping quarters, dining hall, administrative building, recreation hall, and chapel or prayer hall. There were also some smaller sheds and garages for tools and mechanical equipment.

As the doors opened, they were greeted with open arms from many of the followers of Reverend Sun Yung Sun. Spike was happy to get out of the van, but Sebastian was told that he would have to keep Spike on a leash to avoid disrupting the organization of the compound. All the others were ushered into the headquarters, while Sebastian was taken to a grassy area under a shade tree. He was told he could set up his tent and stay here, with Spike tethered on a rope.

After Sebastian put up his tent, he had an hour before they had to meet in the recreation hall for initial instructions and guidance. Sebastian liked to get a sense about people and places, so he and Spike went for a stroll around the camp, hoping to get a feel of the place. Were people natural and easy, uptight and structured, open or closed? He noticed that many of the inhabitants were busy, either working, reading, gardening, or paying tribute to the Supreme Master.

Sebastian took Spike back to the tent before meeting with the new group at the recreation hall. They were greeted by a few devotees who told all to join hands and pray for the well being and unselfish love of their Supreme Master, Reverend Sun Yung Sun.

"You bathe in the light and receive enlightenment from him, for we are nothing without his pure love and guidance," a devotee told them.

They were then told to report to the dining hall for lunch and further information, including a schedule of duties.

Work schedules were distributed, and everyone split up for different duties. The devotees were very careful to keep people apart as much as possible, and each new recruit was always under the tutelage or guidance of a missionary convert. Too much conversation and questioning was not something the organization accepted. Clearly, this was their time to weed out the unfaithful, ungodly, and most importantly, the heretic who dared to question their values and try to create disharmony amongst the group.

Sebastian closely observed the group's methods as he worked in the dining hall kitchen preparing potatoes, carrots, peppers, celery, and beans. Whether he liked their religious beliefs or not, Sebastian did respect their work ethic, thrift, and regard for cleanliness.

Sebastian learned from overheard conversations that Reverend Sun Yung Sun would separate women and men into different properties. He then would arrange marriages between different recruits, sight unseen. The grooms and brides would not meet until the ceremony. Sometimes he would marry 800 couples at one time in a big arena. This was his way of not just marrying them, but also uniting them as a group belonging to his church. Sebastian knew he didn't want any part of this.

The evening dinner ended with a service filled with prayer, proselytizing, and a lot of platonic hugging. Making people feel like they belonged was an important aspect of the agenda. Not a bad thing, if one's intentions were righteous. Most of the young zealots' intentions were righteous, for they themselves were true believers.

The weekend proved to be unexciting. This version of spirituality was not Sebastian's cup of tea, so he asked for a lift into town on Monday. After asking a series of questions about his desire to leave, the devotees declared his convert potential not sufficient and agreed to drive him to the highway. Many would agree that he was smart to leave.

Chapter 14

Free from the constraints of the compound, Sebastian and Spike headed up Route 101 toward Oregon. After a couple of rides, they were waiting on the side of the highway in Ukiah, California, when a police patrol car made a U-turn, sounded his siren one time, and pulled over by them. He asked them to get in the back of the patrol car. Sebastian complied. They were taken to the local police station. Once inside, the questioning began.

"Who are you, and can I see some identification?" asked the officer, a surly, short, plump, middle-aged man. He was balding in the front with slight gray at the temples and had thick eyebrows, which hadn't been trimmed in months.

"Sure," replied Sebastian as he handed over his driver's license.

"What are you doing here in California? You know, we don't like hippies around this town."

"I'm not planning to stay around here. Just passing through," replied Sebastian.

"Did you know hitchhiking on the highway is illegal? Punishable by a fine or jail time or both."

"No, I didn't officer."

After many minutes of being badgered, Sebastian noticed another policeman, a little taller, with bars on his shirt collar, listening and watching.

"Did you know that jail time can also be given for vagrancy?" sneered the officer.

"What exactly is vagrancy?" Sebastian innocently asked.

"It's not having much money or a place to stay."

"Well, we have got some money and a tent to sleep in."

"I'm not sure that will be good enough. It would just be too bad to spend time in jail and have your dog sent to the pound," the fat officer said with a smile.

Just then the taller officer walked over and interrupted by saying to Sebastian, "Did I hear that you were just heading north?"

"Absolutely," said Sebastian.

The taller officer told the other to put them in the patrol car, take them to the city limits, and let them out, and to make sure they headed north. The fat officer didn't like that order, but the chain of command didn't leave much room for discussion. This was one police order that Sebastian didn't mind at all. The thought of Spike going to the dog pound was totally out of the question.

They returned to the patrol car, backpack and all, and rode in silence to the city line. Sebastian wanted to say something sassy to the cop, but he felt it was best to leave things alone and just get out of there, which he soon did.

He wasn't back on the side of the road but a minute, when a caravan of cars passed by. In the lead van, a friend of Sebastian's looked out and saw Sebastian and Spike. He shouted "Holy shit!" and told the driver to immediately stop the van. John jumped out, gave Sebastian a man hug, and asked if he wanted a lift. Unbelievable as it may seem, this was the caravan that'd had no room for Sebastian and Spike at the beginning of the journey. His friend John kept saying "What a coincidence." They talked and laughed together, and John suggested that he stay with the group while they camped in Oregon.

The Ford Econoline van had been customized into a nice travel van. Besides John, there was a collegiate brunette named Jacqueline. She had green eyes and teeth that sparkled when she smiled. Also in the van was a cute blonde girl named Corre. Driving the van was Justin, a big guy with an early receding hairline.

They were part of a seven-vehicle caravan on a vegetative and geological exploration worth almost a semester of credits. They were heading up near Crater Lake in Oregon, where they would spend the next couple of days in a campground. They explained to Sebastian that Crater Lake was just what the name implied, a huge crater left eons ago, and it was part of their scientific study.

Sebastian was well received in the van. Jacqueline and John came in the back and sat by him. Jacqueline immediately started petting

Spike. Sebastian was very inquisitive about their journey and what other sites they had studied.

"What are you doing out here, anyway?" asked Jacqueline.

"The same as you, except we are not getting any college credit for it," replied Sebastian.

"Aren't you scared?"

"Not really. Most people are pretty nice. Just like you."

"How do you know that I don't have other motives behind my innocent smile?"

"I just go on my gut feelings about people and faith in my own karma."

The conversation continued all the way to Crater Lake. Along the way, the driver looked back and said that they had checked with their professor.

"He okayed it if you and Spike want to stay with us for a while."

When Sebastian gave Justin a confused look, he held up a walkie-talkie.

"We have several sets of these so we can communicate between vehicles."

Sebastian was happy to have some company and gladly agreed to stay with the group. Late in the day, they pulled into a campground next to a cow pasture a few miles from Crater Lake. They put up camp in a place called The Rim Ranch. It was a nice campground with a swimming pool, showers, and fire sites with benches around them. There was also a baseball field, volleyball court, and a few horses for trail rides. The group had reserved a large campsite, so they circled their cars like in the old wagon days and set up camp in the middle. Everyone began to scurry out of their vehicles, happy that the long day's car ride was over. They were eager to stretch out their legs and socialize with the rest of the group. Spike was happy to romp around the campground, also. At the professor's order, all began to gather wood for the night's stay.

Sebastian joined Jacqueline in the wood gathering. Since he wasn't sure of his place, he asked John where he should set up camp.

John shrugged. "Anywhere you want. Next to me, or Jacqueline, if you like."

Many of the people in the group went right to the swimming pool after setting up camp. Others were more interested in playing volleyball. Of course, Spike also became a focus of attention. Sebastian joined the volleyball. He was quite good at spiking and blocking, but he didn't want to be too competitive, since it was just a fun game. The games went on for a couple of hours, with teams and individuals switching sides often.

"Are you very hungry?" Jacqueline asked Sebastian.

He nodded. "What are you having?"

"I think we're having burgers, dogs, corn on the cob, and salad. We kind of eat as a group. Everybody pitches in together for the meal, and we divvy it up as fair as we can. Of course, the guys generally eat a lot more."

"I'll have some corn and salad if you don't mind," replied Sebastian.

"Aren't you gonna have any meat?" said Jacqueline.

"I don't eat any meat."

"Why not? And how long have you been doing this?" she asked.

"A couple of years ago, I decided to change my life. I quit smoking cigarettes, started running long distance, and quit eating meat. I guess you would say it was a life-changing time for me. I have since lost about 35 pounds. I have to admit, by not eating as much, it's much less costly for me," said Sebastian.

"But why? And don't you miss it?"

"Why? I was meeting a lot of people who were interested in bettering their lives through healthy, spiritual living, and many were vegetarians. I soon began to feel better with the food that I ate. Plus, it gave me more energy. And yes, at first, I missed eating meat and still do sometimes. Certain foods smell and look delicious. The worst part is when someone invites me for dinner, not realizing that I'm a vegetarian. Then I have to gently tiptoe around the eating situation, so as not to hurt their feelings or offend them."

"I can't imagine not eating steak. Especially when it's on the grill with baked potatoes. I mean, I grew up with meat and potatoes at just about every dinner."

They talked at length while Spike watched the grill hoping for an accidental dropping of food. He managed to win the hearts of many of the students who missed their own dogs at home. In the long run, he got a lot of scraps.

As the sun set, the students built up the campfire and began to roast marshmallows. Sebastian liked them very toasted—black on the outside and mushy on the inside. He and Jacqueline fed each other playfully. A few other couples were also pairing off in playful, flirtatious behavior.

Beers were passed around the campfire, and a group of campers began their own concert, singing both on- and off-key. More campers joined as more alcohol was consumed. The flirtations eventually got more serious for a few of the couples, and they retired to their tents.

"I guess it is getting a little late," said Jacqueline.

"I suppose. That seems to be the general feeling. It's been a long day," said Sebastian as he held her hand.

He leaned over to give her a kiss goodnight, and she wrapped her arms around his neck, pulling him against her body and passionately kissing him back.

"I've got to go wash up," Jacqueline said, as she headed to the ladies' washroom.

"That sounds like a great idea. I haven't washed in a while."

They both cleaned up and went back to their respective tents and tried to sleep. After a while, Spike sensed something at the entrance of their tent. He didn't bark but rather wagged his tail. Slowly the zipper on the screen went up and Jacqueline crawled in. Sebastian was just about asleep when he felt a soft caress on the underside of his neck. Then, in an instant, she was crawling inside his sleeping bag. Sebastian smiled and clutched her closer to him. As their passions rose, she pulled his t-shirt off and then his cut-off jeans. Sebastian slipped his hand under her t-shirt only to find no bra to unhook. Gradually, they both were in the buff, kissing and rubbing each other in their most sensitive areas.

Eros was in the air, and passion had its way as they playfully enjoyed each other's sensual side. Sebastian was a little surprised by the intensity of the emotions that Jacqueline was displaying. He suspected that maybe she hadn't been with anybody in a while. She was a long way from home, with somebody she probably wouldn't see again. Evidently, there was no holding back. Her smooth skin rubbed Sebastian, leaving him with a sensual pleasure that transcended any words she could have spoken. Their breathing increased with each caress, until mutual climax ended the romantic episode. They then drifted off to sleep.

Sunlight filtered into the tent, warming up the cooler night air as the morning arrived, waking Sebastian and Jacqueline. Spike was ready to get out of the tent, and Sebastian promptly attended to him. The day was going to be a busy one. The class had some assignments to complete regarding the flora and fauna of the area. Plus, there had been talk the night before of having a huge softball game that afternoon. The campground's ball field had a backstop, bases, and even a couple of benches on each side.

Everyone chipped in and made breakfast by the campfire: flapjacks, home fries, eggs, toast, and hot coffee. They had come prepared and were organized as to the meals. The group had a whole kitchen set of plates, pots, pans, tools, and silverware as well as a few coolers that they kept filled with ice to keep everything from spoiling. Sebastian had some granola with milk from a cooler.

As he ate, Sebastian watched the group spreading out in the campground, pasture, and the nearby running stream. They were looking for biological specimens to identify and report. As the class did that, Sebastian got very comfortable in a hammock tied to two oak trees in the shade and read *Narcissus and Goldman* by Hermann Hesse. He liked this book. It featured two very different personality types who lived totally separate lives, and yet each admired the other's lifestyle and lived vicariously through the other's stories and conversation.

The hours passed quickly, and before Sebastian knew it, the class had completed their assignments and were ready for lunch. Spike had the run of the campground. Not only was he mooching off the students, but he was also making his way around the rest of the campground, getting sympathy from each couple and family there. He would walk over with his wagging tail and friendly eyes, practically handing each person a card saying "feed me." There were a few other dogs in the campground that Spike got to hang with: an Irish setter named Rojo that was so hyper she had to stay on a leash and, just across the dirt road, a basset hound named Bodacious. (When asked about the name, the owner replied, "His testicles were huge and practically dragged on the ground, so the name seemed appropriate.")

A few of the students picked some mushrooms from under the

cow manure, washed them off really well, and mixed them in with some of the lunch food. They forgot to tell Sebastian that these were "magic mushrooms," which cause mild hallucinations when eaten. So, after lunch, while Sebastian was laying in his hammock, the sky seemed to change like nothing he had ever seen before. It was beautiful, pleasant. Clouds floated by forming figures and murals in the sky. Sebastian had a smile on his face and was in no hurry to play softball. Jacqueline, who also ate some of the same mushrooms, got into the hammock with Sebastian and they laid there for a long while looking at the sky, listening to the radio play music by groups like Cream, Quicksilver, Moody Blues, and the Allman Brothers.

"How long are you going to stay with us?" asked Jacqueline.

"It depends on how long you stay here," replied Sebastian.

"I think we leave the day after tomorrow."

"I guess that is when I will leave. If I remember correctly, your group is heading back south to California. Is that correct?" asked Sebastian.

Jacqueline nodded in agreement.

"Spike and I will be traveling north to Coos Bay and Eugene and Portland."

Jacqueline sort of understood but didn't like it anyway.

"I guess I'll have to make the most of the next day and a half." She began to kiss Sebastian on the ear.

After a while, the softball game got started. With many of the students still feeling the effects of the mushrooms, nobody really cared if they missed the ball. In fact, it became a laughing matter. The game was a comedy of errors.

The group was heading up to the crater in the morning, so the night was spent cleaning up. Some students prepared their daypacks, others took notes for the class. Jacqueline called home on the payphone collect to let her parents know she was all right and enjoying herself. Then she came back to Sebastian. They went for a walk with Spike down the road to a grocery store, where she bought a bottle of Mateus Rosé wine. Sebastian bought some dog food for Spike and some trail mix and apples for the hike the next day.

Everyone sat around the campfire playing word games, singing songs. Some were drinking beer, others wine, and others rolling their own special cigarettes before taking a walk near the pasture. Soon, each returned to their respective tents, some individually, others in pairs.

Jacqueline and Sebastian caressed each other tenderly, his hands artfully circling her body with just enough pressure to titillate her nerve endings. With each circle, she felt her body respond appropriately. From there, he placed his hands on her inner thighs, gently massaging them, while he kissed the underside of her neck. She began to writhe with excitement, yielding to his passionate advances. Her writhing soon brought out a quiet moan, being careful not to let the nearby tents hear. She then pulled Sebastian above her, kissing him gently, pulling him closer. She wanted to tell him how much she cared for him, but she knew better. This was just a temporary arrangement. They continued their passionate encounter, and then quietly rolled off to sleep in each other's arms.

The next morning, the group had breakfast, put on their daypacks and hiking shoes, and piled into the vehicles for the short drive to the Crater Lake parking lot. Their professor paid the special rate for the class. They began their hike up to the rim, which circled the lip of the crater. The crater was a deep pit in the ground that was filled with water, which had to be very cold. The class began to hike around the crater looking for rocks, dirt, and anything that could be studied and examined. Sebastian stayed at the back with Jacqueline and Spike until Spike started to run down the inside of the rim where most people would not go.

It was steep, with no vegetation to hold on to. Sebastian called to him, but Spike started digging. He dug and dug, making a sizable hole, until he had dug up what appeared to be a piece of a large tusk. After several minutes of trying to bite it, he dragged the two-foot piece of tusk to Sebastian, who gave it to the professor in charge. If this were real, it could be a miraculous find. The professor ran down to the park ranger, who called the The University of Oregon Archeology Department and asked that someone come to Crater Lake right away.

Later that day, a team of archeology professors and students arrived with a lot of equipment for digging and examining. Of course, the park ranger had to call his superiors to get the okay for the dig. After what seemed like hours, the park ranger, Richard Murtaugh, finally got the go ahead from the higher-ups in Washington on the condition that the archeological finds would be the property of the Smithsonian Institute. This disappointed the University of Oregon crew, since they would have liked any verifiable fossil to be displayed at their own museum.

Professor Stanley J. Kreiger, the senior member of the group from Oregon, came up and introduced himself to Sebastian and Professor Michael Blackman, the biology teacher in charge of the trip. Professor Kreiger asked to be called Pete. He was a rather tall, erect man about 47 years old, with thinning blonde hair, blue eyes, and a neatly trimmed beard. He wore blue jeans, work boots, and a University of Oregon t-shirt. His eyes were set deep in their sockets and his chiseled face revealed high cheekbones. Sebastian got the sense that he was an efficient, hard-working man who would not tolerate any nonsensical behavior.

He introduced his team to the class and then aggressively asked many questions about the find. He wanted to know of everybody's whereabouts and what dirt had been touched. He especially wanted to know what Spike had done, when, and how. Sebastian showed him Spike's find, which brought a glitter to Pete's eyes. Prior to his arrival, the group had posed, with Spike in the middle and the tusk on the ground in front of him. They had taken several pictures—Polaroids and 35 mm.—including a couple of just Spike with the tusk.

Soon, the area around the find was cordoned off, and the archeological group methodically began their slow but steady investigation. This was going to take a long time. They had tents set up nearby with lights so they could pursue their dig without any distractions. These people had years of experience at this, but it was not going to be easy. The slope of the crater was going to inhibit their movement.

Somehow, word got out about the find, and a newspaper man from the *Portland Daily* arrived later in the afternoon wanting a story. The biology students took turns giving their view of what had happened. Then he interviewed Sebastian, asking about his background and Spike. He wanted to know more about their personal lives and how they ended up with this class. He took more pictures, taped the conversations, and thanked everybody for the information.

It was getting late. Professor Blackman asked the class to return to their vehicles and head back to the campground. Everybody gathered up their belongings. Back at the camp, they all headed straight to the showers to wash off the grime from their dirty trek.

"Crater Lake was truly a beautiful place," said Jacqueline.

"It certainly was. I would have liked to explore the rim more than I did, but after Spike found that tusk, it was just a whirlwind of activity that, in some ways, ruined the day. I actually was hoping to spend more time with you," said Sebastian.

Jacqueline beamed at the sound of those words. She put her arms around Sebastian and kissed him on the lips. Sebastian receptively embraced her and returned the affection.

After everyone had showered, they got back into the vehicles and drove about twelve miles to a restaurant called The Crater Rim Creekhouse. It was a custom-built log building adjoining the national park property. The back of the restaurant had a deck overlooking a creek that was a good thirty yards across. It was a good trout fishing stream, and freshly caught trout was often a specialty on the menu. Professor Blackman had reserved a couple of big tables on the deck for the class.

The menu had a variety of items. The usual sandwiches, burgers, appetizers, and entrees were listed. Being close to the coast, there were several fish entrees, as well as steaks, prime rib, and chops. They also had a vegetarian section, which Sebastian was happy about. The soups and salads were served in custom-made bowls that resembled a crater. Many of the students ordered burgers and steaks, and a lot of the girls ordered salmon and trout. Jacqueline ordered prime rib, medium-rare, with a baked potato. Sebastian ordered ratatouille with brown rice.

The talk of the table that night was the tremendous scientific find that Spike had made. However, Professor Blackman would get much notoriety from the fact that it was his class that had pulled it off. There were several toasts over beers that evening.

Everyone enjoyed the meal, but they were ready for their sleeping bags, after such a long day. Spike was very happy to see them come back, especially since many of the students had saved scraps from their meals for him.

Jacqueline once again crawled into Sebastian's tent, and they spent their last night together.

The next morning everyone packed up their gear, loaded their vehicles, and said their goodbyes to Sebastian and Spike. Since they were headed south to California and Sebastian and Spike were headed north toward Eugene and Portland, he asked to be dropped off near the highway.

The caravan stopped at a supermarket off the highway. Inside, they saw the headline of the *Portland Daily:* "Dog Finds Prehistoric Fossil at Crater Lake" with a large picture of Spike underneath. Sebastian just smirked at the picture. The supermarket nearly sold out of the papers as each student wanted one. As the caravan pulled away, they waved goodbye. Sebastian saw tears running down Jacqueline's face, tears of joy and sadness all in one.

Chapter 15

Once again the two were on the road. Anxious to get back to the Pacific Ocean, Sebastian and Spike got a ride in a pickup on Route 138 to Roseburg, Oregon. From there, a construction worker in a red Volkswagen took them to Coos Bay, on the Pacific. Spike couldn't wait to get in the water. Sebastian just enjoyed the smell of the salt air and the sounds of the ocean waves breaking. The water was a little chilly, but it appeared to be a nice place to hang out for a day or two. There was a campground nearby for bathroom use, and as long as nobody bothered them, he could set up a tent on the beach. When needed, nature provides.

Sebastian and Spike lay by the light of the moon, resting up for the journey to come. Sebastian tried to jot down on a little note pad many of the events that had happened to them so far on their trip. Generally, they went to sleep at dark, but the moon was so bright that night that they found it comfortable to stay up. Because they didn't have a campfire and were back against the trees, they were difficult to see, but they could view others on the beach.

First, a car pulled up nearby, and several teenagers came running on the beach. Sebastian knew they were young by their youthful demeanor, use of language, and activity level. They started running into the water up to their ankles, and then they got in a circle. Sebastian saw a couple of matches lit followed by cigarette embers. He quickly got downwind scents of their smoking, which he knew wasn't Carolina tobacco. Their laughter got louder. Then someone brought out some kind of pipe, which they all shared. Pretty soon, the laughter subsided, and each zoned out on the ocean for a while. After about an hour, they all retreated to their vehicle and drove off.

About fifteen minutes later, a couple, with arms around each other, walked along the beach. They put down what looked like a quilt and then promptly laid down. Sebastian heard the sounds of two pop-tabs open and saw the couple each lift a drink to their mouths. Giggling soon followed, along with disrobing. He then saw the woman pull the man on top of her. The distance was far enough that Sebastian couldn't really identify the individuals. The two were really enjoying each other's company when something moved in the woods behind Spike. He suddenly barked loudly. The sound shocked the couple, who thought they were alone on the beach. They quickly put their clothes on and ran to their car. Spike ran to the woods but came back without anything. Sebastian and Spike went into the tent and slept soundly until the light of the morning sun awoke them.

Sebastian quickly ran to the campground, showered, used the toilet, filled his canteen and Spike's bowl with water, and came back to the beach. He and Spike took a walk back to the highway, bought some fresh fruit, granola, and a few cans of sardines for protein. A short time later, Sebastian took off his shoes and started running up the beach with Spike. Sebastian hadn't been running very long, but his light weight and thin frame made it a little easier to run long distance. He enjoyed running, and he wasn't the only one. The running boom had just hit America, sparked by Frank Shorter's recent silver medal win in the marathon at the Munich Olympics.

Sebastian and Spike had been running for about ten minutes when this guy with shoulder-length hair and a mustache flew by them like he had wings on his feet. Later, when Sebastian and Spike had just gotten back to the tent, the same guy came running by on his way back. He looked over, stopped, walked over to them, and warned Sebastian that camping was not allowed on the beach. He was very gracious. He then asked if they were the ones who had found the mammoth tusk at Crater Lake. Sebastian acknowledged the incident.

"I read that article in the Portland newspaper. It was a pretty cool article. I recognized your dog from the picture, and it did say the two of you are traveling around without a car. So, putting two and two. What a great deduction, don't you think?" He laughed.

"You have got us dead in our tracks. My name is Sebastian, and this is Spike." Sebastian put out his hand, which the thick-browed, wiry guy gladly shook.

"It's a pleasure to meet you. I admire what you are doing, but it's not my kind of life. For me, it's achievement that I strive for. Hey, where are you going from here?"

"We were planning on going north toward Portland. Do you have any other suggestions?" asked Sebastian.

"Well, I'm just visiting my relatives here, but I have an apartment in Eugene. You can hang out there if you want. We like to party. By the way, my name is Steve, but most people just call me Pre."

"Actually, that sounds like a great idea," said Sebastian. "Do you have any pets?"

"No. I like them, but I'm traveling too much to be tied down. But some of my friends have dogs, cats, birds, and whatnot. I'm going back to my relatives' to have lunch and pack up, and then I'll pick you up in a few hours."

"Excellent. We will be ready and waiting," said Sebastian.

They waved goodbye to each other. Sebastian wondered whether Pre would return, but something told him that this fellow would keep his word.

The sun was not quite directly overhead when Sebastian saw Pre waving for him to come up to the parking lot. Sebastian grabbed his pack and tent and hurried along to see a convertible sports car waiting for them. There wasn't much room, but they managed to fit and off they went. Spike loved sitting in the back seat of an open convertible. His ears were blowing in the wind, and the look on his face said "I'm loving this."

"I think it's pretty cool the way you just pick up and go. No goals, no schedules. Like a feather in the wind. I'm just the opposite, driven by goals, schedules, and the need to fulfill my dreams of accomplishment at all costs. Although I'm not exactly a stick in the mud. I do like to party a little," said Pre.

"What exactly do you like to do or achieve?" asked Sebastian.

"Well, I like to run. Or rather, I like to win. Anything else is not an option."

"What events do you run?"

"I run several events, mostly in the middle distances. My best event is the 5000 meters. I really like to front run. You know, lead the pack. My coaches keep telling me that I should be more tactical and hang back with the pack until the last lap, but that is just not me. I believe you don't know what you can achieve unless you give it your all, from start to finish. Anybody that wants to beat me is going to pay for it," said Pre.

"Those are some neat looking shoes you are wearing. I've never seen any like them before. Are they a new brand?" asked Sebastian.

"My coach has been experimenting with the soles. He makes these waffle soles in his kitchen and glues them to our shoes. They feel great, and they grip the track well. They're especially good for cross country and trail running. He and a former Oregon runner recently expanded a small company. I think it might do well. I may just have to invest a little money."

"Are you a religious guy, Pre? I mean do you pray before each race, and ask for God's help for victory?"

"Absolutely not. Do you really think God cares whether or not I win a race? I'm not an atheist or anything, but I believe in myself. God gave me my soul, brain, and the ability to think and reason, so I believe that he leaves it up to us to make our own decisions. I mean, I believe we know right from wrong and what morals we should live by. Therefore, when I make a decision, its coming from within. I believe that a spark of God exists within all of us. Does that make any sense?" asked Pre.

"You make a lot of sense. In fact, I agree with your way of thinking. I've tried to follow different paths of faith, yet I keep coming back to the idea of an inner spark inside me that tells me what is virtuous and what is not. It's not what people say or call themselves, but it's something much deeper, that you can't put words to. Yet, when you see it, you know it exists," said Sebastian.

Pre nodded. "How about going for an easy trail run today? I need an easy pace today because I'm racing the day after tomorrow. It's only about a five-mile loop. Can you run that distance? Even Spike can come along."

"I can probably make it if you run your absolute slowest pace."

They put on their running shorts and shoes. Sebastian had a pair of Adidas cross-country shoes, and Pre had those homemade shoes given to him by his coach. Sebastian was much taller than Pre, with long, bird-like legs, and his recent trip and being a vegetarian had really taken away most of his body fat. They started easy, jogging down the trail, talking as they went, but gradually Pre's competitive spirit took hold, and it took everything Sebastian had to keep up. Finally, Sebastian called out ahead for Pre to hold up and wait for him.

"I'm sorry. I just get into the run, it starts feeling good, and I want to go. I forget that you are not a competitive runner. I'll be on my best behavior the rest of the way."

During the remainder of the run, they discussed interval training, fartlek running, and the use of hill repeats to improve one's fitness and ability. Distance running in America was just beginning to boom, as well as other types of activities and self-exploration.

Later that evening, Pre and Sebastian—Spike stayed back at the apartment—drove around Eugene, the university campus, and, of course, the mecca of running, Hayward Field.

"This is where it all happens. This is where I turn men into boys." He smiled. "Once you step out onto the track, it's no longer friendship and politeness. It's literally a war, with the spoils going to the victor. We all have good and bad days, and times will vary depending on the weather, season, and whatnot. However, it usually comes down to who wants it the most. It's not just who is the most fit or has the most speed. It's the one who is willing to go into oxygen debt for the longest time to win it. Although, some people are peaking at different times, that can have an effect, also."

"What do you mean by peaking?" asked Sebastian.

"Peaking is the training regimen taken to have a runner at his fittest for a given race distance at a certain date or time of year. For instance, if a runner wants to peak for the Olympics, which usually takes place in July or August, their training regimen will be different in the winter and spring than it would be in early summer. They may be working on their distance base in winter and early spring, not worrying too much about speed. But as spring begins to unfold, they may start to run shorter distances at a faster pace to increase their overall times. They do this so that they have peak performances for the national Olympic trials, and continue through the summer, hopefully reaching their best shape at the Olympics," explained Pre.

"Are you peaking now?" asked Sebastian.

"I peaked for the track in the spring. Now I'm increasing my distance and trail running for some cross country races in the fall. However, when you love what you do, you often always feel like you're peaking."

They ended up at a bar in Eugene. Since Pre was a celebrity, the brews were flowing for Pre and his new friend. Sebastian was happy since he didn't have much money to spend.

In the morning, Spike was anxious to get outside, so he started pawing Sebastian to let him out. Sebastian had a slight hangover, and as he opened the door, he felt a light mist falling on him. He was glad he was staying in an apartment today and not standing by the highway. He browsed the bookshelf and saw an array of books, both contemporary and classics. Several interested him, especially a few on religion and metaphysical reality.

Sebastian tried to keep abreast of international politics and the craze of the day, yet what really interested him were the ideas that don't change with generations, ideas that can withstand the tests of time and values. He believed that truth is based on a value system, and since values change with time, so do our truths. So, someone who is ahead of the general public in understanding a value is often ridiculed or even destroyed. Yet, later when the masses come to understand that value, he often becomes a posthumous hero, or a martyr. Sebastian wanted to submerge himself in the truths that most civilizations have held dear, and those truths that will always be held virtuous. He also wanted to steer clear of values that some civilizations held dear but that are not virtuous, at least in Sebastian's eyes.

"Good morning. What are we going to do today?" said Pre, as he stretched his arms and then pulled on his moustache.

"Whatever you want to do is fine with me. After all we are your guests."

"I say we have some female company today. Is that all right for you?"

Sebastian just nodded his head.

Pre smiled. "I have a wonderful lady friend who has a lot of girlfriends, and she even has a dog for Spike to hang out with. I'll give her a call."

Later that day, the rain stopped, so Pre, Sebastian, and Spike got into the sports car and drove about ten miles to a suburban house that was surrounded by woods. They got out and were greeted by three pretty college co-eds and a little border collie named Sugar. Spike was right on it, sniffing her butt like any good dog would. Introductions were made by Pre to Sally, Jenny, and Marti. They all had nice smiles and were very pleasant, which made Sebastian feel more comfortable.

After a few beers, the girls fired up the grill to cook some burgers and chicken. When they asked how Sebastian liked his meat, he replied, "Invisible."

They laughed, not quite understanding. Then Pre informed them that Sebastian was a vegetarian. The looks of laughter suddenly changed as if an alien had arrived in their house.

As the evening wore on, they forgot about Sebastian's strange dietary habits and got along fine with him. Of course, Spike and Sugar were cozying up very nicely. Alcohol always seems to loosen people up and make them friendlier than they usually are. The beer that day was no different, and Sebastian and Spike felt totally welcome and at home.

Waking up the next morning with a slight hangover, Sebastian took a few minutes to get fully awake. After showering and feeling better, he walked into the living room and immediately sensed a change in Pre's demeanor. He was serious, focused, and pacing the room.

"Why are you so intense today?" asked Sebastian.

"Today is a race day, and I take racing very serious. Today is the first cross country race of the season. This will be different because it will start in town, go out on the local running trails, and finish up at Hayward Field. It's almost like a combination road, trail, and track race all in one. I don't really care what they call it. Running is running. Doesn't matter much the surface, as the best man will win anyway."

"How can you race after drinking beer last night?"

"I was just carbohydrate loading, man, enough to carry me through the finish," said Pre with a smile. "After the race starts, walk back to Hayward Field with the rest of the crowd, and I should be back in thirty minutes or less. I will be hard to miss because I'll be the first one in the stadium and crossing the finish line."

"How can you say that when you don't even know who's running against you?" asked Sebastian.

"It doesn't matter. I want it more than the next guy, and I will back up my talk with the victory."

Sebastian knew this guy was good, and clearly he was also very confident in his ability to run. Pre told Sebastian that he had to warm up and mentally prepare for the race a few hours early and that he would drop Sebastian off on campus. He could either hang out at the student center or go to the library until race time.

Right before noon, the runners started gathering around the starting line. There were probably 250 runners, which was a lot for this kind of race. Most of the runners were high school or college age. However, there were several older runners, who looked almost as fit as the younger ones. The starter had a pistol, which fired blanks and made a loud noise, starting the race. Pre was wearing number one and, of course, was in the lead after only a few hundred yards.

Sebastian walked back to Hayward Field, and not long after he got there, a lone runner entered the track with no one on his heels or even close behind. The small crowd started chanting "Pre, Pre, Pre" and clapping. This locality was very knowledgeable about running and appreciated the sport in itself. After circling the track, Pre flamboyantly crossed the finish line in 29:07 at least two minutes ahead of the next finisher. As he crossed the line, he put up two fingers spread apart for the sign of victory. He was a man of his word.

After the race, Pre explained that he had some previous engagements that day and would be unable to be around, but that Sebastian and Spike were welcome to stay at the apartment. However, Sebastian put out his hand and thanked Pre for graciously giving them shelter and friendship during their stay. He told Pre that he would look in the papers and follow his races whenever he could.

"Where are you going to now?" asked Pre, as he twirled his mustache.

"Probably up north toward Portland."

"What's up there? Anybody you know?" asked Pre.

"No, it just seems like a good destination."

"I don't know how you do it. I mean, just casting yourself in the wind with hardly any money and a dog and not worrying about anything." He shook his head.

"I guess you just have to have faith in God, yourself, and your fellow man," answered Sebastian.

"I know one thing, Sebastian. You have given me a view of life that I haven't really thought too much about or experienced, but it's been good meeting you and Spike."

Pre helped them with their bags and drove them to the entrance of the northern side of Interstate 5. As he took off, they waved goodbye. That would be the last time Sebastian would see Pre.

Chapter 16

Spike and Sebastian sat along the highway for about an hour before a pickup truck with an older husband and wife told them to climb into the bed of the truck. They hopped in and got dropped off on the outskirts of Portland. They didn't get a chance to talk to the couple but graciously thanked them for the ride.

It was approaching evening, so Sebastian asked the gentleman if he knew of a campground nearby. The man pointed north and said to go two miles and head east, that there was a state park about five miles down on the right. They walked the two miles, and then caught a ride to the state park. Sebastian decided to wait until the office closed and then sneak into the campground. They would find a lonely spot of grass and set up his tent. In the meanwhile, they sat on the grass by a big open space where a group of young people were playing Frisbee. One of the guys asked Sebastian if he wanted to play. Sebastian had work boots on but agreed to play. They were playing Frisbee like you would play touch football, except they were using a Frisbee. After playing a while, the game broke up, and the guys mostly hung around talking about their new jobs and new faith.

It seemed that all of these young guys were born-again Christians who, after years of living a negative lifestyle, had been saved, and now they gave their lives to serving Jesus. These men were all in their mid- to upper-twenties, mostly college educated, white, and from the northwest part of the United States. They were asking Sebastian the usual questions about himself, his origin and education. Most were curious about his religious beliefs. Sebastian kind of beat around the bush, preferring to learn about their faith while avoiding any confrontation. Before leaving, they invited Sebastian to a church picnic the next day. Sebastian agreed, so they said someone would pick him up the next day at noon at the entrance to the park.

Ten o'clock rolled around, the office closed, and Spike and Sebastian quietly walked into the campground. About fifty yards from the washrooms was a nice open spot for Sebastian's portable tent. Anxious to take a nice cool shower and fill his canteen with water, Sebastian didn't waste any time. As luck would have it, there was a small freshwater stream running not too far from their tent, so Spike could get cooled off and get a drink for himself.

The morning sun awoke Sebastian. He quickly washed and toileted, packed away his tent, and left the campground before they opened up. He hid his pack in some bushes near the entrance to the park. He and Spike then took a walk down the road to a market, where he purchased some fresh fruit, a small bag of dog food, sardines, a quart of orange juice, small jars of peanut butter and honey, and a small loaf of whole wheat bread. They walked back to the park, had breakfast, and waited till noon when they were supposed to be picked up by the guys from the Frisbee game.

A few minutes before noon, a Chevrolet Impala pulled up, and Sebastian could see a couple of the guys from the previous night. The driver asked him to hop in the back seat of the car. It was a light blue Impala hardtop with dark blue seat covers and white wall tires. Spike climbed in first and then Sebastian.

The driver turned and put out his hand. "I'm Jay. Glad to make your acquaintance. This is Rick."

Jay had brown hair that was just over ear length, a fair complexion, and some dandruff specks over his navy blue polo shirt. He had wire rim glasses that gave him an educated look. Rick appeared to be about 6 feet 3 inches tall and 210 pounds. He was clean shaven with close-cropped dark hair. He wore khaki pants, brown penny loafers, and a white button-down shirt. Based on his muscular build, Sebastian thought that he might have played football in college.

They drove about ten minutes and arrived at a small, well-kept church with a steeple. There was a parking lot and a playground behind the church. The parking lot was filled with cars. As they walked around the back, they saw many young families with small children running around and playing on the swing sets, seesaw, and the climbing bars and slide. Sebastian could smell fresh meat cooking on the grill. He knew that once again he was going to have to explain why he didn't eat meat. Many of the guys from the Frisbee game came up and greeted him, while many of the youth went to pet Spike.

"Where can I leave my backpack and tent?" asked Sebastian.

"You can leave it in the recreation room of the church, outside the kitchen," said Rick.

Sebastian did as he was told and returned. Shortly thereafter, it got quiet, and all of the members gathered in a large circle, joined hands, and bowed their heads in respect to the Lord. Their minister, Reverend Grady, was a middle-aged balding man of small frame and short stature. He wore dark rim glasses and had thick, dark eyebrows hiding behind those dark rims. He held out a Bible and read a passage from the New Testament. Sebastian heard a lot of "Amens" and "Praise the Lords." After laying the Bible down, Reverend Grady thanked everyone for helping make the previous year an exceptional one and announced that the designs for the church expansion were already underway due to the excellent fundraising and tithing that everyone had done all year. Everyone applauded.

He then looked over to Sebastian and said, "We have a welcome guest. Let us show him what hospitality our Lord Jesus can offer a lonely traveler in his time of need." He then walked up to Sebastian, hugged him, placed the Bible over his head, and said, "Jesus, bless this young man and his dog for the rest of their journey, and help him find the way to the Lord."

The congregation shouted, "Amen."

Sebastian asked if he could help with the meal. He didn't have any money to give, but at least he could give his time and labor. Sebastian shucked corn and then switched to slicing tomatoes, onions, cucumbers, celery, and carrot sticks. He saw Jay and Rick helping out with the huge grill. They had hamburgers, hot dogs, chicken, and a few ribs barbecuing. The food did smell good and delicious, yet Sebastian had made a commitment not to eat meat, at least for the present time in his life. During the food preparation, many of the church members came up and introduced themselves to Sebastian.

When everything was about ready, all gathered again, heads

bowed. Then, Reverend Grady once again held the Bible to his forehead and affirmed the glory of God. With controlled emotion, he extolled the virtues of living a life with Jesus, and only by being saved, by giving one's life to Jesus, can one be with God when the rapture comes. After a harmonizing "Amen," he said grace.

The congregation responded, "Praise be the Lord."

All began to distribute the food, first to the children, then the teenagers, and finally to the adults. Spike was around, as usual, looking to grab a loose morsel whenever he could. Sebastian had no doubt that Spike would walk away with a full belly by the end of the meal. Everyone was gracious to them.

Every couple of minutes, someone would approach Sebastian and ask if he had a congregational connection, or if he had found Jesus. Sebastian said that he was searching for his true beliefs and was open to learning. Well, that just left the door open for a lot of proselytizing.

Sebastian thought about much of what they said about their devout Christian beliefs. He already followed much of it to a T. However, he never felt his belief system could be so cut and dry. Something inside him always resisted when someone or something said "Follow me: my way is the only way." On the other hand, following these beliefs was a beautiful thing, if done in the true spirit of Christian beliefs. Yet, according to these Christians, living with these morals and beliefs was not enough to reach heaven if one did not also put one hundred percent faith in Jesus.

After the meal, a Frisbee game started up behind the church. This was apparently a popular sport for the group. Sebastian watched for a while before he was approached to join the contest. Sebastian asked if Spike could play, and they agreed. Of course, who could catch a springer spaniel at full speed? They started to send Spike downfield on hike, and then throw it long. All they would see was this brown and white blur downfield. Then, Spike would leap into the air, catching the disc across the goal line. Spike was the hero of the game and earned some leftover potato salad and dried up hot dogs.

After everyone got a little tired, a few members got out their musical instruments: acoustic guitars, flute, and mandolin. They began to play and sing songs, mostly Christian with some folk songs thrown in. While they were singing, Reverend Grady came up to

Sebastian and motioned for him to come sit back under a tree away from the group. Sebastian followed.

"Sebastian, you seem like a nice individual who is trying to find his way. Am I right or wrong?" asked the minister.

"I guess I would have to agree with you," replied Sebastian.

"Well, from the bottom of my soul, I would be doing you a disservice if I didn't try and acquaint you with the teachings of the Lord Jesus. I would be remiss if I didn't give my very best to let you feel the true love and brilliance of the Lord Jesus."

Reverend Grady talked to Sebastian for more than an hour, and Sebastian quietly listened and answered most of the questions as well as he could. He thanked the minister for taking the time to spread the Word.

"I will earnestly dwell on what you taught me today."

As the singing came to an end, many of the people were starting to leave. Sebastian stayed to the end, helping to clean up. They told Sebastian that he could pitch his tent on the church property for the night, or someone could give him a lift within local driving distance. Sebastian thanked them graciously and asked to get a lift back to the park and campground where he had stayed the night before. It was comfortable and safe, and he had full use of the toilet and showers there.

One of the men in the group came up to Sebastian and placed a small cross made out of wood into Sebastian's palm. "Whenever you are in need, place your faith in Him, our Lord Jesus. He will see you through your difficulties." The man then quickly left.

That night Sebastian thought a lot about the good people of the church, their devout faith in Jesus, and their kind-heartedness. He thought it would be a lot easier to just follow a dogma and give yourself completely to it. Yet, something inside prevented him from doing just that.

The next morning Sebastian and Spike caught a short ride to Portland, Oregon. They walked around, looked at the Willamette River, viewed Mt. Hood in the distance, and enjoyed the fountains and parks of downtown Portland. He was sitting on a bench, watching the business people of Portland go about their hurried way when a man in a pin-stripe blue suit, white shirt, blue tie with white dollar signs in a design approached him. He wore black silk socks and black Italian shoes that had the shine of a sergeant-major in the army. His neatly trimmed hair matched his well-manicured nails. He appeared to be in his forties but looked very healthy for his age.

"Are you out searching for the meaning of life?" the man said to Sebastian.

"Something like that," Sebastian replied.

"Twenty years ago, I was doing something similar, just in a different era. But I finally found my God."

"Really? And what is your God's name, and how did you find him?" asked Sebastian.

"He found me actually. It was a time of dire need, and he appeared, giving me the bread of life, shelter from the storm, and a philosophy to heed for the rest of my life."

"Sounds like a pretty powerful event in your life. Do you ever doubt your God or his powers?" asked Sebastian.

"No, I don't. I just enjoy what I have been given, and try to make the most out of it. My name is Charles Colbert. And yours?"

"Sebastian, and this is Spike."

"I've got two dogs myself, a Chesapeake Bay retriever, and a German shorthaired pointer. Spike would probably get along with them."

"You haven't told me the name of your God," said Sebastian.

The man smiled. "So, you are curious about my God."

"Kinda," said Sebastian.

"I see you have a backpack. Do you have a place to stay tonight? Don't worry, I'm not homosexual or anything. I just want you to have the chance to know my God, same as I did twenty years ago."

Sebastian just looked at him, quite surprised at the invitation, but also quite curious. He didn't sense any real evil in this man, like the kind that might do bodily harm to him. So he stood up, shook the man's hand, and said, "I guess that would be okay."

"I will call my wife and let her know that I'm bringing two guests home." The man then walked about twenty yards to the pay phone on the side of the building and made the call. He then walked back to Sebastian, and said, "I just have to clear up a few things at my office, and then we can go. Wait here. I will be back in about 45 minutes."

Sebastian wasn't sure if the man would return, or if he was on the up and up. So he just stuck to his faith in karma, that everything would turn out all right. Sure enough, 45 minutes later, Mr. Colbert appeared and motioned for Sebastian and Spike to come with him, which they did expeditiously.

They walked about a quarter of a mile to a parking garage. He opened the door to a brand new Mercedes-Benz sedan. This automobile had all the bells and whistles, with leather seats to boot. He draped the back seat with a quilt before Spike got in, and they put Sebastian's backpack in the trunk. Sebastian had never ridden in a car like this. This was the top of the line in luxury automobiles.

On the way to Charles's house, Sebastian was looking out at the beautiful Oregon scenery, wondering what the night had in store. They drove a while as the city gave way to suburbs, and the suburbs gave way to more rural areas. They approached a gate which shielded a long driveway leading to a beautiful mansion. The sleek, black Mercedes glided into a garage as big as some people's homes. Sebastian and Spike jumped out of the car, Sebastian got his backpack, and they exited the garage via an elevator that opened up into a foyer off the main great room. Sebastian was in awe upon seeing this one part of the mansion. The great room had windows on three sides, creating a feeling of being outdoors. The home overlooked the grassy banks of the Columbia River on one side.

"Quite a view from here, don't you think?" said Charles.

"Absolutely amazing. Everything. The house, the environment, the furniture."

Sebastian spun around and saw Mt. Hood looming in the distance, like a majestic lord guarding its magnificent domain. Just then the door opened and two dogs came running in, first the Chesapeake Bay retriever and then the German shorthaired pointer. The Chesapeake was a big, brown, curly-haired dog with a big chest. He must have weighed close to ninety pounds. The pointer was gray with black spots and looked strong.

"The retriever is named Diamond, and the pointer is called Gold."

"I see you enjoy the symbolism of their names," said Sebastian.

"It's not just the symbolism. When the change in my life came, I decided to recognize everything that has become me and to embrace it rather than hide it."

Sebastian heard footsteps that sounded like a woman's heels. He turned and saw a beautiful brunette walking into the room. She was about 5 feet 9 inches tall, 130 pounds, and her thin frame was draped with a turquoise blue dress revealing a little bit of cleavage with each bounce of her step. Her olive skin was contrasted by the shiny white pearl necklace encircling her sultry neck. Long, pearl and turquoise earrings dangled from her small, thin earlobes. Complementing her necklace and earrings was a turquoise and gold bracelet on her right wrist and a few gold bangles on her left. The final piece of the showcase were the gold and diamond rings on her fingers.

"This is my wife, Samantha. I'm quite the lucky man to have such a lovely, intelligent woman willing to share my life," said Charles.

As Sebastian took a step forward to shake her hand, Samantha came right up and gave him a loving hug.

"Anybody that my husband deems worthy to bring home to our humble abode truly has my full welcome. Please make yourself right at home."

In the meantime, Spike was hesitant in his approach with the two bigger dogs. They sniffed each other, and then the tails went from straight to wagging, a sign of peace. Samantha let all the dogs outside.

Sebastian took a closer look around and saw magnificent pieces of furniture, original works of art, and decorations that had to come from around the world. Even with such eclectic items, it all flowed together.

"Did you have your house designed by a professional interior decorator?"

"Actually, Samantha handpicked and arranged everything. See I told you what a jewel I have. Samantha will give you a tour of the house, and then we can sit and talk for a while before dinner," said Charles.

Sebastian followed Samantha into each room in the house, noting the expensive decorations and designs. The kitchen had all the most modern conveniences, a true chef's paradise. The family room had a Brunswick pool table, poker table, pinball machines, and even a dart area. There was also a special room just for viewing movies, with comfortable chairs lined in rows. They continued on to the dining room and bedrooms, which were as exquisite as all the others. Samantha had immaculate taste, but Sebastian wondered whether she had really put this all together herself, or whether she had had some help from an interior designer. Each room had a theme, whether it was a color or ethnic flare or designer influence.

After Sebastian and Samantha returned to the great room, Charles suggested they sit out on the deck and have a drink.

"Do you drink alcoholic beverages?" asked Charles.

"Not too often, but I'm not averse to drinking alcohol," answered Sebastian.

Samantha pushed a cart, which was essentially a rolling bar, out to the deck. It had various bottles of liquor lined up on ledges around the outside of the cart. They all had pourers on the top. On the bottom side was a wine cooler that plugged in to the nearest outlet. On top was an ice bucket and another cooler filled with non-alcoholic mixers such as orange juice, tonic, ginger ale, and mixes for sours. Around the sides on another ledge were glasses of different sizes and shapes. Adjacent to the ice bucket was a cutting board, paring knife, and various fruits.

"Ladies first. What would you like, Samantha?"

"I'll have a martini, please."

Charles poured the gin and vermouth, mixed it with bitters and an orange peel, and gently handed it to Samantha.

"What would you like, Sebastian?"

"I'll have whatever you are having?" replied Sebastian.

"You are taking your chances, but I won't steer you wrong. Since we are having fish tonight for dinner, I have a very nice German white wine from the banks of the Rhine Valley."

He pulled the cork from the bottle and poured Sebastian's glass and his own almost full. Sebastian wasn't used to drinking good wine. His experiences were mostly limited to Liebfraumilch, Mateus, Blue Nun, and Riunite. He savored the smooth taste and enjoyed what he was drinking. The more he drank, the looser he became, finding conversation a lot easier and overcoming the feeling of awe he had in this mansion. The sound of dogs barking disrupted their conversation, so Samantha opened a gate to let the dogs onto the deck.

"I've got some chores to do, so I'm going to leave the two of you to discuss whatever, without female introspection," said Samantha, as she went back inside.

Charles and Sebastian sipped their wine and played with the dogs, who were getting along great, with no territorial problems. Then Charles became very focused, asking Sebastian to listen and engage him in a more serious conversation, maybe even one that could have life-changing possibilities. Sebastian nodded his head and directed his attention away from the dogs, toward Charles.

"Sebastian, what have you been doing on this trip? Have you been searching for yourself? Maybe searching for God?"

"Something like that. Maybe a little of both," replied Sebastian.

"Some people's idea of God may be red, as in the political and economic philosophy of Communism. Other's idea of God may be blue, as in the fulfillment of our lives as a reward in heaven. However, my idea of God is green."

He pulled out a dollar bill and handed it to Sebastian.

"This, my friend, can achieve on earth what no other ideal or purpose can. It can bring you comfort, peace of mind, security, health and welfare, and even political power. The ironic thing is that by achieving wealth, one is able to perform more charitable acts than by being a member of the ministry. Do you know that more marital problems come from economic difficulties than any other? Money may not bring happiness, but it sure eliminates many of the obstacles in the way of happiness. Money brings the freedom to do what you want to do when you want to do it instead of having to work at some crappy job while trying to squirrel away enough money to finally do what you want to do. What I am trying to impress upon you is that the world is your oyster, but you must focus on cracking that shell open. Inside that shell is the world of wealth. I want you to take a few minutes to think about what I just said."

Sebastian took a few minutes, leaning over the deck railing, looking at the Columbia River, dwelling on the recent conversation. He turned and approached Charles, sitting back down and addressing him.

"Why did you invite me here? Obviously, we have nothing in common. I'm just a young guy with no money or real ambition, and you have this high-powered life with wealth, a beautiful wife, and plenty of drive."

"Maybe I see in you more than you see in yourself," said Charles.

"What do you mean? Please explain that statement."

"Well, after World War II, with the expansion of the transportation and the hospitality industries, America was growing in leaps and bounds. I was one of the early Beat Generation. I didn't know what I wanted, so I took off around America working odd jobs here and there, searching for myself. Actually, something like you, except that we had shorter hair back then."

"You traveled around hitchhiking like me?" asked Sebastian.

"Yes, but without a dog. I probably spent a couple of years here and there just making ends meet, but then I experienced a life-changing situation."

"What was that life-changing situation?" asked Sebastian.

"I met a man who had grown up as a sharecropper in Mississippi. He talked slow, didn't look like the sharpest nail in the toolbox, but he had a goal and stuck to it. He picked me up one day and started telling me his plan to earn his fortune. He had a plan called 'Dare to be wealthy,' which he was about to put into action. He said that if I would help him generate his product, he would give me a free membership in the organization. Since I didn't have any money to contribute, my donation would be time and effort, which I agreed to," said Charles.

"What was this business about?" asked Sebastian.

"It was about making money. It was really a scheme to get rich on people's basic greed. It was a pyramid operation."

"What's a pyramid operation?" asked Sebastian.

"Well, you sell memberships to people for a certain amount of money. In turn, when they sell memberships to other people, they get some of the money, but the largest part goes to the top of the pyramid which was Eugene and myself. So, to join, each member had to give five thousand dollars, and then they would get their greedy friends to join, and they would get a cut. Ultimately, everybody made money as long as the pyramid kept growing. It's only when it stopped growing that the bottom layers wouldn't earn anything."

"Is that legal?"

"Maybe not now, but back then some things in the law were left alone. It was something else. We would wear American flags on our lapels, drive Cadillacs, mink ties, and the most expensive suits. When we had our meetings, we would hype up the event. Members would do cartwheels waving the American flag. We didn't allow people to have a negative thought. Everything was focused on getting rich, and to get rich, they had to join right away. We even took them on nice vacations. I got my first taste of money then."

"How long did you do that?" asked Sebastian

"For a few years, but then legislation began to break up pyramids, so I decided to take my money and invest in other areas. You see, once you have money, it's easier to make money. I'm telling you this because I see a bright guy in you, but one who hasn't made his life's choices yet. We all eventually make those choices, and once we do, it's hard to change course, especially after wives and children get involved. Don't get me wrong about God, I still believe in living a moral life with respect to others, and I feel there might be an afterlife, but for right now, living the wealthy life takes priority here on earth."

"I understand what you are telling me, but I'm not sure I totally agree with the whole concept of wealth being the end all, be all," said Sebastian.

"What's not to believe? Where have most of the charitable donations in this country come from? From the wealthy industrialists. The Carnegies, the Vanderbilts, and the Rockefellers. People don't realize that the only reason the poor and lower-middle-class hate the rich is because they are jealous and envious of their lifestyle. Probably 99 percent of the lower economic classes would live the same way if they could. It's only that one percent, the *idealists* who might not choose wealth, because they have this unrealistic view of the way life should be. It's a grand utopian vision of life at it's best. Unfortunately, it will never happen because the vast majority fall prey to their lower traits, one being greed."

"Much of what you say makes sense. I just need more time to dwell on the concept and evaluate its merit in comparison with other visions of life."

"And you will. When that day comes, if you would like to work with me, in one of my companies, come look me up."

Sebastian and Spike spent the night, enjoying the wonderful hospitality of Charles and Samantha, living the material dream. The next morning, they said their goodbyes and continued their journey.

Chapter 17

Sebastian and Spike weren't on the road very long when an eighteen-wheeler pulled over. The driver opened the door, said he was headed to Reno, and asked if they would like a ride. Sebastian nodded, grabbed his pack, put Spike in the truck compartment behind the driver and passenger seats, and then got into the passenger seat himself. The ride through the Oregonian landscape was beautiful. They traveled down Route 5 through Eugene, Grants Pass, and Medford, before crossing into California and finally arriving in Reno, Nevada. Sebastian and Spike were dropped off at a truck stop along Route 80. Sebastian used the facilities, filled up the canteen, and gave Spike a bowl of food and water. It was early in the morning, about 3 a.m. Sebastian was running low on money and thought it was time to head back east to regroup and earn a little cash.

One of the waitresses at the truck stop told him she would be leaving work at 6. She was going as far as Winnemuca, Nevada, if they wanted a ride. Sebastian agreed, anxious to leave the fumes of the truck stop. She introduced herself as Aida. She was a widow, 48 years old, and had two grown children, both living in California. She'd had a hard life. She hadn't finished high school and her husband had been a painter who only worked seasonally and missed a lot of days due to his heavy bouts of alcohol abuse. This left Aida to be the main provider for the children as well as the caretaker for most of the household duties. He eventually died from cirrhosis of the liver. She didn't say it, but she must have had some relief after his death. She looked a few years older than her age—wrinkled face, graying hair—but she had a kind heart and enjoyed serving people from out on the road. Driving Sebastian and Spike was kind of a cathartic experience. She could empty out all of her psychological problems and air all of her frustrations, regrets, and grievances to someone who was willing to listen but would never see her again. Sebastian appreciated the ride and was happy to be of service. He had some experience, having worked as an aide in a psychiatric hospital for a short time. He mostly listened and repeated back to her some of her main concerns, letting her expound on them.

"I appreciate you letting me talk about my life. Sometimes I just don't have anybody to talk to, and it just wells up inside. Sometimes it gets so bad, I get these terrible headaches. I think they call them migraines."

"I'm sorry to hear that. Don't you fret at all. Talk all you want. It will probably do you a lot of good. Keeping stressful things all balled up inside you will probably shorten your life."

"Why, you are just such a nice boy. I wish my daughter was around here to meet you. She's working in Fresno, California, waiting on tables. She ran away at 16, met this trucker, fell in love, and don't you know, he left her six months later. Now she's trying to get her life together. She's still only 22 years old, but doesn't have any education, or really know what she wants to do. She's a really smart, pretty girl. I just don't want her falling into the same trap that I did. You know, falling in love with someone who ain't worth a lick, who doesn't even care if his wife is the main provider. A man like that ain't no man as far as I'm concerned."

"What are your daughter's goals? Does she want to do anything special with her life, besides wait on tables?" asked Sebastian.

"She has mentioned several times, she would like to work in a hospital, but doesn't know how to go about it. You got any ideas?" asked Aida.

"As a matter of fact, I do. If she would like to work in patient care, she could initially work as a nursing assistant, and if she likes that kind of work, she could go back to school to be a nurse or X-Ray technician. There are lots of career possibilities in the hospital. If she doesn't want to work directly with patients, she could get a job as a unit secretary or one in medical records, and if she likes it, go back to school for administration. Plus, there are also food related occupations in the hospital. However, if she has ambitions to do more, insist that she go back to school, or think of some business idea she could start. Most important, if she is not happy, don't let her settle for anything that doesn't bring her some self-worth."

They continued on, with Aida doing most of the talking and Sebastian nodding a lot. Spike was snoozing in the back seat of the Chevy Chevelle. She showed Sebastian some pictures of her daughter and he agreed she was pretty. She later confided to Sebastian that her husband had abused her daughter. She had suspected it but wasn't sure until she was older. By the time her daughter told her, he was terribly sick. When he died, she wasn't sorry at all. She said that wasn't how family life was supposed to be but guessed that many things in life aren't what they are supposed to be. Sebastian felt pretty bad hearing this, but he knew it was good for her to get it off her chest. He figured she didn't have the money for a shrink, and it would be embarrassing to tell a friend that she had suspected child abuse but didn't do anything about it.

As they got near Winnemuca, Aida felt very relieved to have gotten much of her pain out in the open to someone who would listen. She wanted to do something for Sebastian.

"Sebastian, I don't have any money, but I'm a damn good cook. I want to cook you a great meal before you go off on the road again, and I won't take no for an answer."

"All right, but I have to tell you that I don't eat meat. Can you still make a great meal?" asked Sebastian.

"You betcha! As a matter of fact, there have been many times when I didn't have any money for meat, and we made do with what we had," replied Aida.

They drove into a poor section of Winnemuca and came to an old run-down house. It was a white, wood ranch house with a little front porch. The wood needed some painting. As they walked through the doorway, Sebastian noticed that the room had limited furniture and decorations, but it was neat and clean.

Aida said, "I'm sorry I don't have a nicer place for you to visit, but I've never had much money. My husband never earned very much. Just about everything came from waiting on tables." Aida kept talking the whole time she was gathering up the fixings for his meal.

"I thought that we would have money after his mother died, from a life insurance policy she carried, but he told me that she declared his sister the sole heir. We were surely disappointed because we could have used some of that money." She took out a bunch of cans from the pantry and some baking goods from the cupboard and started whipping up a meal.

"Would you like a drink or something? We still have some scotch or whiskey left over from my husband's cabinet."

"No, thank you. I'm not much of a hard liquor drinker, especially in the morning."

"That's about all that no-good-for-nothing left me with, besides a bunch of medical bills."

The time passed and Aida kept talking as the kitchen started to smell good. The old stove still worked well enough for baking and cooking. She made a nice yellow cornbread square with jalapeño peppers, and a Southwest-style bean casserole. It had chili beans, pintos, and black beans mixed with crushed tomatoes, peppers, some corn, and a nice mix of spices. She served the casserole in bowls with writing on the side: "Nevada Where the West Stays Wild." By now, Sebastian was quite hungry, and this surely hit the spot. He must have liked the cornbread, because he ate five pieces.

During this time, Spike was out in the backyard sniffing around, when suddenly a tabby cat ran into the yard. Spike started chasing it, and the cat ran into the detached garage, squeezing itself under the door. Sebastian and Aida heard a lot of scrambling around, hissing and barking. It got quiet for a moment, and then all they heard was barking.

"Do you think we ought to go see what's going on?" asked Sebastian. "What's in that garage, anyway?"

"Just a lot of junk my husband kept in there. He never liked me to go in there. Said it was a man's place, just as the kitchen was mine. As a matter of fact, I haven't hardly been out there since he died."

They opened the garage door to an old broken-down car. There were also a lot of rusty tools, empty liquor bottles, a few pinups of Marilyn Monroe, and a lot of other worthless items. Spike ran straight to a corner and started digging. There appeared to be a hole in the wood floor that had been covered with a board and old carpet. Spike had started digging away the covering, and as they got close, the tabby cat jumped out, ran between Sebastian and Aida, and out the door with Spike following. Aida walked over and picked up a large Whitman's candy tin that was in the hole. She tried to open it, but it was closed pretty tight. She asked Sebastian to try.

"Why would he keep this hidden in the ground? I hope it isn't pornography, or pictures of him cheatin' on me with some hussy. Although I wouldn't be surprised if it was. It would be just like him to do that," said Aida.

Sebastian struggled to open the tin and finally pried it open with a screwdriver.

"What's in it?" asked Aida.

Sebastian's eyes opened wide, and he handed it over to her. Inside were stacks of big bills, twenties, fifties, and hundreds. With the money was a letter from Omaha Life Insurance company: Dear Mr. John Mcginty, you have been designated the sole beneficiary of the life insurance policy of Beulah Mcginty. Enclosed is a check for $50,000.

"Why that son of a bitch. He was keeping this money for himself and lying to me about it the whole time. I told you he was a good-for-nothing. The only good thing about this is that the bastard died before he had a chance to spend all of it on gambling, liquoring, and whoring at those brothels downstate." She looked at Sebastian. "How much do you think is still here?"

"I'm not really sure. That's the most money I've ever seen in my life."

They both looked around the rest of the garage, but nothing else was of much value. They went back in the kitchen and counted the money. It totaled just under $39,000. Aida finally started smiling after ten minutes of cussing her departed good-for-nothing husband.

"I'm rich! And it's because of your dog, Spike. Your dog has made my life a hell of lot easier."

Sebastian went back to finishing his casserole and cornbread, but Aida was too excited to eat. She just kept saying that Sebastian deserved a reward for his dog finding it.

Sebastian shook his head and said, "My reward is seeing your life become a little less stressful. If you really want to give a reward, though, we could go to the grocery store and get Spike a box of dog biscuits. That would be reward enough."

Sebastian encouraged her to take that money and immediately put it in her bank account, which she did on the way to the store. After going to the store, she dropped Sebastian and Spike off at the on-ramp of Interstate 80, heading east. They waved goodbye, Sebastian feeling really good that he got to experience the joy and life-changing opportunity for such a sweet lady.

Chapter 18

Waiting on the Interstate 80 ramp in Winnemucca in the summer was a very hot experience for Sebastian and Spike. As the sun climbed into the overhead position, the temperature must have been 110 degrees or more. Sebastian was wearing work boots, but Spike's paws were feeling the heat from the hot tarmac. He started whimpering. Sebastian gave him as much water as he could spare and held him like a baby for as long as he could.

Luckily, a white van pulled up. Inside was a middle-aged woman and three children of various ages. She stopped and took a quick look at Sebastian, who was holding the springer spaniel. He walked around to talk to her through her open window. She asked where he was going, and he said east.

"I want you to know, I'm only stopping because I feel sorry for the dog, not you," said the woman.

Sebastian just smiled. "I'll take the ride any way I can get it."

"Do you drive and have a valid driver's license?"

"Yes, ma'am. Here it is." Sebastian showed her the license.

"My name is Krystina Perikowski, and these are my children, Peter, Jonathan, and Mary. We visited Disneyland, the San Diego Zoo, Hollywood, and San Francisco. We are now heading back to our home in Chicago. It's a very long drive, and I would like to drive straight through. We could take turns driving, if you don't mind," said Krystina.

"No, I don't mind, but you don't even know me. Aren't you worried?" asked Sebastian.

"I read people well, and I saw the way you were holding your dog. I think we will be safe with you."

Sebastian and Spike got in the van. The kids were all over Spike, and he loved the attention. Krystina had some fresh water for both of them. Although the drive was long, it was on one interstate most of the way. They would learn a lot about each other during the ride.

The Perikowskis were a devout Polish Catholic family from Chicago, Illinois. Krystina was a first-generation American, born in the United States. Her parents had left Poland in the mid-1930s. Her father had been a chemist in Warsaw. He had seen the build-up of the Nazi party in Germany to the west and the total supremacy of the Communist party to the east in Russia and saw the writing on the wall. It was a very smart move, since a couple of years after they left, the two countries would make a non-aggression pact in order to divide up Poland between themselves. He had liquidated his assets and taken his family first to London, then to New York, and finally to Chicago, where he landed a job as an assistant professor at the University of Chicago. His specialization was creating new molecules for better and stronger materials.

Krystina grew up in an ethnic neighborhood in Chicago, surrounded by women wearing babushkas and long dresses, and men wearing the drab clothing of their past. The aromas of kielbasa cooking in a delicious sauerkraut and bacon casserole and stuffed cabbages baking in the oven would drift out the apartment windows, seeking out every nostril on the street. The languages spoken on the street were a mixture of Polish, Russian, German, Slavic, and a host of other dialects. The children often became the interpreters for the parents, who had emigrated for the good life in America.

Krystina's father, who was better educated than most of the immigrants, moved out of the neighborhood after the war ended. With the suburban boom growing, her father moved a little farther out, to a house with a lawn, garage, and all the accoutrements of a successful family living the good life in America. Over the years of the '50s, '60s, and now the '70s that suburb became swallowed by the city and was just another ethnic neighborhood in Chicago, inhabited by later generations of Europeans.

"So what are you doing out here in the middle of nowhere letting your dog burn up in this midday sun?" asked Krystina.

"We are on our way back to Pennsylvania. We have been out west for months, and now it's time to regroup back home for a while," replied Sebastian.

"Are you a religious person, Sebastian? I mean do you believe in God, morality, and a heaven and hell?"

"That's pretty complicated for a one sentence question. But I'll try to be completely honest with you, even though I'm still working on answers to all those questions as we speak."

"That would be nice since we are traveling with you, and I am entrusting the care of my children to a stranger who will be driving my vehicle. You see, we are devout Catholics who live according to the teachings of our religion. And if your morality doesn't mesh with ours, maybe we should part ways."

"I do believe in God. It's just that my faith is a work in progress. My beliefs generally don't conform to any man-made religion. I believe that I'm a much more moral man than most would perceive me to be. I just think that religions separate people and cause dissension. I believe we are judged by our actions, not by our verbal commitments. I think that we make choices in life, and once we are mature adults, we must endure the consequences of our actions. I think God looks after children and fools, but if we know better and still choose evil, a punishment is in store for us at some point in time."

"You really have done a lot of thinking about God. I guess we just accept what we have been taught and live by our faith."

"Did I pass the test?" asked Sebastian.

"It's not really a test, but I have a lot at stake in this vehicle. I just wanted to know where you are coming from. You can rest now. I'm pretty sure you aren't some anonymous serial killer, and that goes for your dog, too."

So, they got along well, and agreed to continue traveling together to Chicago.

Driving through the Rocky Mountains and the Great Plains to Illinois was going to be a long haul. They continued along Interstate 80 through the great state of Wyoming and the cities of Laramie, and Cheyenne.

As they were approaching Cheyenne, one of her kids yelled out, "Mom, I just saw a sign for a big county fair with a rodeo! It's happening today. Could we go? Please?"

"I hear you, Jonathan. There's no need to yell. Peter and Mary, would you like to go to a county fair and rodeo?"

"Absolutely," replied Peter, as he and Mary nodded their heads.

"Sebastian, would you like to go to the fair?"

"Only if they let me take Spike in on a leash. It's too hot to leave him in the van for most of the day. Otherwise, Spike and I will be on our way."

"Well, I wasn't planning on a long stop like this, but we have some time before we need to get back home, and since everyone wants to go, we will go."

They pulled off the highway and found their way to the fair. When they got out, Sebastian talked with the security guard at the gate and asked about putting Spike on a leash. The guard, who had a few dogs himself, said that it would be all right, but he probably wouldn't be able to sit in the stands at the rodeo. He and Spike would have to stand by the fence to watch. That was just fine. Sebastian thanked the guard.

After walking through the entrance, they could see different food stands selling hot dogs and sausages, lemonade, pizza, ice cream, and a host of other foods, including funnel cakes. After the food was the agricultural hall, where the prize vegetables were on display. One gourd weighed hundreds of pounds. There were also champion tomatoes, squash, and cucumbers. The preserve and jam judging was taking place, and there were many free samples available to the general public, with homemade bread to boot. Sebastian saw little boys and girls with jam all over their faces.

Going through the agricultural hall didn't take too much time. They then went to the barnyard area to see the miniature horses, sheep, chickens, and prize cows and bulls. The bulls were a major attraction because a prize bull's sperm is very valuable to a cattle rancher. There was a greased pig catching contest taking place for kids under thirteen. Sebastian laughed as he watched the little ones fall over one another trying to catch the slippery pigs.

At the end of the fairgrounds were the rodeo grounds where cowboys competed in events such as roping and barrel racing. The most exciting and dangerous events, however, were the bucking bronco riding and the bull riding. The bulls could weight close to a ton and they would think nothing of trampling or goring a fallen rider. The rodeo had cowboy clowns who position themselves inside the arena when a rider comes out of the chute. When a rider falls off of a horse or bull, the clowns are there to distract the animal and keep its attention away from from the fallen rider. They also entertain the people in the stands.

The Perikowskis went to sit in the stands while Sebastian and Spike stood watching the events through the rodeo fence. The competitions began with the young riders, as young as elementary school age. Of course, the animals were very young calves and colts. With the increasing age of the riders, came increasing size and aggressiveness of the animals. Between age groups, the clowns would take a rest break until the next rider mounted an animal. Then, they got into their positions.

Toward the end of the competition, an especially angry bull came into the chute. Nobody realized that the gate hadn't latched properly. As the rider was preparing to mount, the bull slammed into the gate, opening the latch and bursting into the open arena. Just as that happened, a man who had been holding his child on his shoulders turned around and the child jumped into the arena to see the bull. With no clowns in the arena and the thousand-plus pound bull loose, the audience began to shout, scream, and cry. Parents in the stands were cringing. When Sebastian realized what had happened, he didn't hesitate to throw Spike into the arena, knowing Spike could at least draw the bull's attention away from the child until help could get there.

In a dash, Spike quickly ran and positioned himself between the bull and the child, barking and growling, showing his teeth at the huge bull. Not that this terrorized the bull, but it did catch him off guard. It was just enough surprise aggression to redirect the bull to another part of the arena. The clowns and other rodeo personnel were out there within seconds of the dog-bull confrontation, but it was Spike who actually kept the child out of danger. Once the child was taken out of harm's way, the audience broke into cheers and applause for Spike and the clowns. The rodeo photographer was already snapping pictures of Spike when Sebastian ran over.

It wasn't long before the local newspaper got wind of the incident, and Spike was the focus of attention. The paper wanted pictures of him with the little boy and invited Sebastian and the Perikowskis to stay the night. In fact, the rodeo administrator wanted all of them to appear on the stage that evening before the country music bands so he could publicly thank Spike. He offered to pay for their rooms at the Holiday Inn, two miles from the fair. Krystina and Sebastian agreed, since the rest might do them all good. They spent the evening at the fair, went back to two rooms at the inn, and enjoyed a restful night, ready to begin their journey to Chicago the next day.

Shortly after dawn, they got up to check out and saw on the front page of the local paper a picture of Spike between the bull and the child. The caption read "Visiting Dog Saves Child from Brahma Bull."

Sebastian shook his head, amazed how his little springer spaniel had become such a publicity hound. Of course, he always knew what terrific qualities his dog possessed. Aside from his parents, Sebastian had never felt unconditional love from anybody. Yet, with Spike he knew that no matter what, Spike was always there for him regardless of circumstances. He had found a bond with the dog that he had never experienced before. Spike was never judgmental, never required quid pro quo; it was just pure devotion, and the only thing required was a little dog food and water.

"That was quite an event last night," said Krystina.

"Yes, quite. Spike really handled the situation well. It was almost like he grew up on a farm, corralling animals. I sometimes think that his intelligence is greater than most people realize."

"I know my children were quite impressed with Spike's actions. In fact, Jonathan said that it's too bad most humans don't possess those traits of bravery and honor. It's a sad state when my child realizes that people don't always live up to expectations," said Krystina.

"Sad, yet very realistic. Many people either don't care or are too afraid to pursue their higher state of being and embrace the virtues that are part of that concept. I think it's good that Jonathan sees the world without rose-colored glasses," said Sebastian.

They continued to head east on Route 80. It was a long boring ride through the wheat fields of Kansas and then the cornfields of Iowa. Krystina began to feel comfortable with Sebastian, enough to confide some of her deepest feelings, problems, and situations. Driving with someone for hours on end, you get to know them and begin to let down your guard. Krystina told Sebastian that she had been divorced for about a year. It wasn't something she was proud of, nor wanted, but her ex-husband, Wlodek, had been cheating on her for a couple of years. She had no idea about the affair. She thought he was away on business trips when he had actually been staying with a woman who worked at his office.

Krystina never suspected anything, until one spring evening when she was taking her kids to a soccer game across town. She pulled up to a red light, and there was her husband's car in front of her, with another woman in the passenger seat. She followed his car until he parked on a residential street. When they both got out and went inside a house, Krystina wrote down the address, and on several occasions, when he was supposed to be out of town, she drove past that house and saw his car parked in her driveway. She hired a private detective who followed Wlodek and photographed and detailed each and every transgression. These photos and documentation became her evidence of unfaithfulness and disloyalty that any court would recognize and grant her divorce demands.

They stopped to eat lunch in Des Moines. The ride through Iowa was uneventful but filled with more personal conversations between Kristina and Sebastian. The dinner hour was approaching, and knowing no food was in the house, Krystina thought it best to stop for dinner. There was an interesting restaurant along the road with a giant figure of a boy holding a huge hamburger. It appeared to be a very kid-friendly restaurant. They had a separate kids' play area. The sun was going down, and soon it would be dark. They proceeded into the restaurant to a table with paper placemats that were filled with questions to answer. There were also diagrams and puzzles and colored pencils to keep the kids busy at the table.

The waitress approached the table. She was about nineteen years old, had long blonde hair, greenish eyes, and stood about 5 feet 4 inches tall. She had a friendly smile. She also had a noticeable scar on the left side of her neck. Sebastian wondered about the origin of its appearance but wouldn't be so rude to ask. Krystina ordered a big beef cheeseburger with onions and cheese, and the kids all ordered hot dogs. Sebastian ordered a grilled cheese from the kids' menu and a glass of water, while others all had Coke. Krystina wanted him to order more, but Sebastian wanted to pay his way.

The conversation encompassed a lot of small talk, as Sebastian surveyed the restaurant population, which was mostly families out for dinner. Sebastian had brought his water bottle and asked if he could fill it up. He excused himself, went outside, and poured it into Spike's bowl before going back for his meal. Krystina did not want to discuss her marital problems with Sebastian while the kids were awake and listening. She was looking forward to finally arriving back home in Illinois. She loaded her burger with ketchup saying that she was happy they had Heinz brand. It was the only kind she bought.

With their bellies full and the day getting late, the kids drifted off to sleep shortly after they got back on the road. Krystina went back to talking about her cheating husband. Sebastian listened and tried to understand the circumstances of her situation. He didn't understand the deception, the lying to someone who you supposedly loved. Of course, he had never had a long-term relationship to base his opinion on. It just seemed not to be the right thing to do. He felt that honesty was usually the best policy. That way you never have to look back with regrets. Krystina had been raised in a strict Polish household where one got married and stayed married for better or for worse. Her husband's seedy behavior and the fact that she would have to get divorced was devastating to her, but it was not of her choosing. She didn't start it, but she was going to finish it.

The highways in the Midwest are like pancakes, flat as can be, and a driver must be careful as it's easy to exceed the speed limit. Sebastian concentrated on keeping a light foot when he was driving. He didn't have to worry as much about deer as back home, but the flatness dulled his senses. He could see that it might lull a person to sleep while driving.

Krystina explained that she had gained ownership of the house and much of the furniture as well as custody of the children. Her ex had visitation rights one weekend a month. He had to pay a nice sum of alimony in addition to child support each month for the three children, but this messy situation had taken its toll on Krystina's emotional psyche. She hadn't been herself since. She thought she had achieved what she had dreamed of, a nice life with a successful husband and beautiful children, but then suddenly no more. She said this trip was helping her rebound and gain more self-confidence.

Sebastian asked about her childhood and what she had been like while growing up in Chicago. She said that she was born Krystina Smolenkowski on November 12, 1942. She said that she had been a thoughtful child who rarely rebelled, accepted authority, and tried to please her parents and teachers. She had always been a strict Catholic who placed priests and nuns spiritually above the rest of mankind. She learned to play the flute and piano, focusing more on classical music than pop. She didn't become valedictorian of her class, but she did excel in academics. She said that she had been socially inept. Being a little too introverted kept her from being one of the "in crowd."

"But I'm not really sorry about that. I achieved what I wanted. Until that horrendous day when I saw him with her. It's just now, while trying to raise three children, I find myself alone and without the social skills to meet new people."

"I wouldn't worry about it too much. I find you delightful to converse with—sincerely. Our conversations have been enjoyable, and you have a pleasant demeanor," replied Sebastian.

Krystina was a little taken aback by his words. She was not used to getting compliments from others. "That's only because you have spent hours with me one-on-one and I let down my guard. Usually with new people, I find it difficult to talk without sounding like an idiot."

"You are being too hard on yourself. Just don't think too much when you meet someone. Don't worry about impressing them. An ideal companion will see through all that anyway. Be yourself and enjoy the moment," said Sebastian with assurance.

"What about you, Sebastian? What were you like growing up?" asked Krystina.

"I guess I was just about everything that you weren't. I was rebellious, didn't study at all, almost didn't graduate high school. I was very social and liked to be in athletics. I have never really actually known what I wanted. I have always liked new experiences that teach and enlighten me. Hopefully, one day, I will know what I want to do with my life."

"I'm sure you will find your way. It takes a lot of guts and personality to do what you are doing. I still can't believe that I actually picked you up. I normally would never do that, but Spike won me over. You are very different from anyone I have ever met," said Krystina.

"That didn't sound too good, like I'm an alien," replied Sebastian.

"No, don't take it that way. Just about everybody that I know wants to graduate, get a good job, marry, have a family, live in the suburbs."

"One acre and security. The suburban American dream. It's a nice life, if that's what you want. I hope that's not for me, but sometimes life has a way of making everyone succumb to standards they previously considered unacceptable."

Krystina was only about five years older than Sebastian, but she had a lot more responsibility in her life. She was feeling more comfortable around Sebastian, laughing and letting out her true personality. This was the first man she had lightened up with since her husband's affair. It felt good to just be herself.

"We should reach Chicago in a couple hours, and then we can finally relax. Sleeping in the car, while the other drives isn't very restful. I appreciate you helping me drive. Otherwise, it would have cost more in motel stays. You saved me some money," said Krystina.

"The feeling is mutual. I'm afraid I might still be out there in Nevada's 120-degree sun if you hadn't picked me up. You saved me from being a dried up raisin. Seriously, I have enjoyed your company, and your children are a lot of fun and very well behaved."

That statement made Krystina proud. The fact that her children were well behaved was a sign that her parenting wasn't for naught.

"When we get to Chicago, I will be more myself and relaxed, when I'm in my own home. Do you have to be anywhere special in the next couple of days? I'd like to show you Chicago," Krystina said.

"I'll have to check my appointment schedule." Sebastian laughed. "That would be very nice."

It was late at night when the van left the interstate. They were headed to the Avondale neighborhood, home to a large Polish population. Actually, the Chicago area had the largest Polish population in the world outside of Poland. This area was northwest of downtown Chicago. Riding through the avenues, Sebastian could see the various Polish stores and the many churches that displayed Eastern European architecture. Instead of the typical American steeple, many of these had a Byzantine or orthodox look. Plus, many of the store and restaurant signs had Polish language letters, advertising various Polish food specialties.

They arrived at a two-story home with a front porch and fenced-in backyard. The exterior was wood, probably built at least forty years before. It was a basic but solid design. Krystina was relieved that they had arrived back home safe and sound after their long journey. Spike was happy to get out of the van and stretch his legs a bit. The kids had been asleep, so their joy to be home was tempered by their drowsiness. When Krystina opened the door, the house had a stuffy smell from being closed off for weeks. Sebastian's initial impression was that this was a very practical and homey environment for her family. Many of the furnishings were not new, and some were even American antiques. There was only one air conditioner, situated in the window of the main living room. The other rooms each had a small fan placed in prime spots to circulate the air.

Krystina asked Sebastian to bring his pack upstairs, and she showed him the guest room where he and Spike could sleep. She then excused herself to get her kids to bed quickly and quietly. Most of the rooms had a ceiling light and one or two table lamps placed strategically in the space. After Krystina successfully got the kids to bed, she showed Sebastian the rest of the house. They talked and agreed that the next day would be busy. She then gave Sebastian a big hug, kissing him on the cheek and thanking him for helping drive and for being a great companion all the way from Nevada. Krystina didn't forget Spike, for he got a big hug, also. Sebastian said good night, and then took Spike out back to do his business before he also went to bed.

"Good morning, Sebastian," said Krystina. "You must have been really tired. The kids and I have been up for two hours already. I hope you don't mind, but I let Spike out this morning and fed him."

"Oh no, I'm glad you did. Thank you. What are the plans for today?"

"I thought that I would give you a walking tour of my neighborhood. Is that okay?"

Once they were all dressed, they took a stroll a block or two to the main avenue, where Krystina showed Sebastian her church. It wasn't very ornate, a simple red brick Catholic church with stained glass windows and a school attached on one end. The school had a little playground. On the other side of the church was the rectory, the living quarters for the priest.

"I had my confirmation here, and hopefully, my children will, too."

Sebastian, Krystina, the kids, and Spike strolled down the avenue in Avondale, stopping in various shops, getting the kids candy, and finally stopping for an early lunch in a Polish restaurant. The window out front had a little lady with a babushka wrapped around her head. They went in for a platter of halushkie and pierogies. Sebastian chose the sauerkraut, while Krystina ordered the potato and cheese. They were covered in fried onions and butter.

"This is the first time I ever had this kind of food. It is very good. Reminds me of an empanada or a ravioli but with a different twist."

The halushkie was basically noodles covered in butter, fried and seasoned to perfection, mixed with cabbage. Adding sour cream to the dish was a wonderful option. While they ate, Spike sat quietly outside the door, patiently waiting.

On the way back to the house was an advertisement for a dance that night at the local hall. Krystina looked at Sebastian and asked if he would like to go.

"Why not?" said Sebastian.

"Good. I'll see if I can get a sitter for the kids. It will be only a couple hours."

Luckily, Krystina was able to secure a sixteen-year-old neighbor who didn't have a date that night. Plus, she didn't mind Spike staying with her. Just before 8 p.m., Sebastian and Krystina walked to the dance hall. It was about a mile away. As they entered the room, which was decorated with red and white banners and had an ice skating rink presence, Sebastian noticed a polka band getting ready to perform. They had trumpets, saxophone, drums, and a couple of accordions. The lead singer was a large, balding, middle-aged man with a big gut protruding over his belt. While Sebastian watched the band, a woman approached Krystina and gave her a hug as if they were childhood friends. She looked to be Krystina's age but thinner and fitter, like somebody who had remained single without the responsibility of raising children. She wore a black skirt, white top, a pearl necklace, and black open-toed shoes. Her dirty-blonde hair was pulled back in a long ponytail. She had the smile and warmth of an elementary school teacher. Krystina introduced her to Sebastian as her best friend's younger sister and explained that she ran the neighborhood recreation center.

Once the music started and the beer started flowing, more people hit the dance floor. The lead singer worked the crowd while the accordions gripped the people, as an electric guitar does in pop bands. Krystina asked Sebastian to dance. He only agreed after a few beers and her teaching him a few steps. This was fun, but it wasn't his personal choice of music. They had a good time, sometimes switching partners with other dancers. It was mostly a blue-collar crowd. The union was heavily represented in this dance hall. As the night winded down, Sebastian and Krystina walked the mile back home. Both tops were wet from sweating on the dance floor.

"I had a great time tonight. Thanks for accompanying me to the dance," said Krystina.

"I had a really fun time, too. Now I can dance the polka. I very much appreciate all that you have done for me since Nevada."

"What are you going to do tomorrow? If you want, we could visit downtown Chicago."

"Thanks, but I think Spike and I will be continuing our journey. We really had a good time with you and the kids, but you have a lot to take care of, and Spike and I still have some traveling to do."

"Spike has been a godsend for the kids. He has such a good temperament with them, and they love playing with him. It's amazing how he can find the ball or stick by just the scent."

The two walked together toward the house like old friends, even though it had only been days. Being together 24-7 brings a closeness like nothing else. They reached the house, Krystina got out her key, and slowly opened the door. It needed oiling, by the creaky sound it made. They sat around after she paid and thanked the babysitter. Sebastian offered to escort the sitter home. It was a shame that Sebastian's and Kristina's age and life experiences were so different, because their personalities complemented each other very well. They watched a late night movie on TV, ate some Jiffy popcorn, and kissed each other good night on the cheek.

The morning brought a bright, warm, sunny day, and Sebastian could smell the aroma of a freshly cooked breakfast. After he got his pack together and bathed, he went downstairs, fed Spike, and then let him out in the backyard.

"Good morning," said Krystina and the kids in unison.

"Are you hungry? We have eggs, bacon, pancakes, and home fried potatoes."

"I'll have a short stack of pancakes, if you don't mind," said Sebastian.

"Where are you going today?"

"Spike and I will go back to the interstate and head east."

As they walked to the street, Krystina and the kids gave them hugs and kisses and waved goodbye. There was a definite sadness in the air while they walked away.

Chapter 19

They hadn't been on the interstate more than twenty minutes when a recent-model, solid black Buick pulled over. The window opened revealing gray leather seats and a large cross hanging from the mirror. In the driver's seat sat a man with closely cropped gray hair. He had a ruddy complexion, wore black shoes, black pants, black shirt, and black jacket with a white collar.

"Hello," he said, in a faint Irish brogue accent. "Where are you headed? I'm going to Toledo, Ohio. Is that all right with you?"

"That's great. It will be greatly appreciated," replied Sebastian. "We are heading back to Pennsylvania; we have been out on a journey." Sebastian and Spike got into the back seat.

"Did you have fun? Did you find what you were looking for?"

"Not quite sure, but it has been very interesting."

"As you probably already surmised, I am a Catholic priest. You can call me Father Ryan. Are you by any chance Catholic?"

Sebastian shook his head. "No. I'm not Catholic, but I am interested in learning new things."

"I wasn't always a priest. In my younger years, I was pretty wild and did some pretty stupid things. But I guess God had a purpose for me, because the next thing I knew I was in the seminary studying for the priesthood."

Sebastian nodded his acknowledgment.

"What, if any, have your contacts been with people of the Catholic faith, if you don't mind me asking?"

"Well, as a young person, I played on sports teams with kids that were mostly Catholic. They all went to parochial schools and wore ties and jackets to school. They didn't talk about the religion too much. Mostly they complained about how the nuns could whack them with a ruler if they stepped out of line. I did go to church a few times, but it was all in Latin, so nobody understood what was going on. As I look back on it, they didn't seem any more spiritual than anybody else."

"What do you know about the New Testament?"

"I believe Jesus spoke out against the ways of the temple, created a following, and was eventually nailed to the cross by Pontius Pilate. Supposedly, he died for our sins. Also, they always said that his mother was a virgin."

"I see you have a basic, simplistic understanding of Catholicism. It gives us a good starting point. If you have any questions, please feel free to ask them at any time, okay?

"As Christians, we have an affinity with Judaism. In the Old Testament, God spoke to the people through the prophets. In the New Testament, He spoke definitively and acted decisively in the life, death, and resurrection of Jesus, seen as the Christ, the anointed and chosen one of God. It is then that early Christianity took its start. The early Christians were Jews. He was their Messiah, whom God had sent to earth, and He wanted them to be His disciples. Before I go any further, do you care or want to hear more about the Catholic faith? If not, I won't continue about this."

"No, I don't mind, as long as you keep it simple and not so erudite and I can ask or debate any point with you."

"Good. I'll welcome any discussion. Keep in mind that not every point can be scientifically verified. Much of what we believe is based on faith."

"Why did people believe that Jesus was the chosen one? Was it because he was a great orator, a leader, or what?"

"There were many reasons that Jesus developed a following. Many would say that since He was the divine agent sent to earth by God, His aura was captivating enough that followers felt the divinity within Him and were compelled to follow."

"Is it possible that his disciples were 'true believers' looking for a cause? I respect your beliefs, teachings, and especially the virtues that you follow, but weren't these testaments written by men? And men are certainly not infallible."

"Christianity has been examined over two millennia by

thousands of extremely intelligent human beings, and they all agree that too much of what has been written in the Testaments was too complicated for man to invent by himself. Of course, much of the Catholic religion is based on faith. You must have faith and believe in Jesus Christ as the son of God, if you want to be a Catholic."

"In the early days of the Catholic Church, wasn't the Pope also the head of a political empire?"

"Not in the early days, but several centuries later that is true. However, you must remember that we follow Jesus, not the Pope. Even though the Pope is the figurehead of the Church, he is but human. A good example might be that even though the President of the United States may be less than honorable, we still believe in the principles of the constitution and the freecoms that America provides."

The car cruised along Interstate 80 toward Toledo, and Father Ryan continued to discuss, probe, and answer Sebastian's questions about Catholicism. Spike just laid in the back seat waiting for the ride to end. The priest asked whether Spike needed to stop for a drink or a rest stop, which was very nice of him. Sebastian thanked him, but the ride from Chicago to Toledo was not that long. Spike could wait until they arrived. Sebastian had some granola with him, which he offered Father Ryan. The priest replied that he was more of a Kellogg's man. Of course, Spike had the look of "What about me?" so Sebastian gave him a milk bone. It was late morning when Toledo signs started appearing on the side of the highway.

"What are you and Spike going to do when we exit the interstate?" asked Father Ryan.

"We probably will go find a supermarket with a bathroom, and then go back to the interstate," replied Sebastian.

"Why don't you two come to my parish? We can feed you there, and we have ample space for guests to stay. We don't usually allow animals, but Spike is so well behaved, I think we can make an exception."

Sebastian thought for a few seconds and then agreed to the invitation. He was grateful to have shelter in the summer heat. The black car exited the interstate and wound its way through city streets. As they rode and stopped at stoplights, Sebastian noticed that the neighborhood started to look economically depressed.

Driving through the various streets, Sebastian observed different ethnicities with each passing block. It was almost as if certain areas were separate enclaves of nationalities. Although the North never had legal segregation, the people themselves tended to congregate with their own. This in essence became de facto segregation. It revealed itself through the types of occupations each ethnic group controlled and the type of graffiti written on the bare walls, shutters, and doors in the neighborhoods. As they drove, beautiful murals appeared occasionally, draping a building's wall or fence. Even the ethnic cooking spewed forth aromas that only one's ancestral cooking could articulate. One could even tell the economic climate of a neighborhood by the number of people just hanging out on the sidewalks and doorsteps. Places where employment was high, the residents had jobs to be at, leaving the sidewalks emptier, and vice-versa.

"How are you doing back there?" asked the well-meaning priest as he peered into the mirror.

"We are doing well. Spike's managing to keep his restlessness under control."

Father Ryan turned the black Buick onto an avenue, which seemed to be home to many religious organizations. Every few blocks, a large building with a different style topping appeared. Some represented Gothic architecture, others Baroque or Byzantine. There were various cathedrals and temples. Many of these places of worship were absolutely beautiful and well designed. Clearly, the builders had not lacked sufficient funds when they were built. But by now the people who built them had reached some part of the American success story and moved out to suburban neighborhoods. Unfortunately, that has been the practice in most American cities. Due to the size of the nation, when people immigrate here, they bond as one group, work menial jobs to improve their economic status, send their children to college, and eventually, by the second generation, they become homogenized into the American culture. They speak English as their first language, move to bigger homes in the suburbs, leave the inner city neighborhoods to the next poor immigrants to take over.

Finally, after driving several miles on the avenue, the Buick turned into a church parking lot. The building was an old gray

Catholic church, with stained glass windows depicting Jesus and the Virgin Mary and Child. To the side of the church was a two-story building which appeared to house a small school and gymnasium. On the opposite side stood a three-story residential building, which Sebastian thought must house the nuns and priest of the parish.

"We are here," said Father Ryan. "Now, don't be bashful to ask for anything that you may need. Get your pack and take your dog to the side of the building. There is a small lawn where he can take care of his business. After that, come through the front door of that brick building. I will be in my office, which is the first door to your left. I will take you and Spike to a room where you can stay. If you are hungry, we have a small kitchen which always has some basic food supplies."

"Sounds pretty good to me," said Sebastian, as he began to walk to the lawn with Spike. While Spike was sniffing the grass and trees, Sebastian noticed some of the buildings had broken windows or boards over them. He then took the priest's advice and walked into the building.

Inside, the walls were a dark mahogany with a light every thirty yards down the hallway. In the middle of the hallway was a painting of the Madonna and Child. Sebastian told Spike to stay in the hallway and then walked into the priest's office. He sat down and began looking at pictures on the wall. Father Ryan must have been quite the athlete when he was younger. There was a picture of him gliding over a bar, pole in hand, and big letters ND on his chest. Another showed him wearing a football helmet with one bar across to protect his face. Again, the letters ND and the number 7 were printed on the side of the helmet. In between those was another picture of the priest, with a full head of hair, in front of the Vatican.

"I have a lot of work today, but you and Spike make yourselves at home. Your room will be the third door on the right. The kitchen is two doors past that. Please stay on the first floor. The nuns are housed on the floors above. Also, keep Spike out of the chapel, which is across the hall from your room. You can go out. There are some stores nearby, a park two blocks up. Just be back in the building by dark. The streets can be pretty rough when the sun goes down. We lock the doors to the building at 9 p.m. Is that okay?"

"You bet. Thank you for the hospitality."

Sebastian and Spike went to their room, which was small and very generic but comfortable. Spike had a little rug to sleep on next to Sebastian's bed. There was one chest of drawers, one chair, and one small sofa. The view out the window was of the houses on the next street over. He was getting a little hungry, so they went to the kitchen down the hall where they found two nuns in their thirties sitting at a table.

"Excuse me," said Sebastian, "but Father Ryan said we could spend the night and have use of the kitchen."

"No problem," replied one of the nuns. With their gracious smiles, they immediately asked Sebastian what he wanted to eat.

Sebastian said, "Peanut butter and jelly would be just fine."

"What about the dog?" replied the taller nun.

"Oh, I've got food for him in my pack."

They presented Sebastian with PBJ on wheat and a glass of milk.

"May we pet your dog?" asked the shorter nun. "It's one of the few things I miss. I grew up on a farm in Indiana, and we had dogs and cats my whole younger life. I remember walking to school with my border collie, Rusty. Then he would run back home when I got to school property."

The taller one chimed in and said, "I had a German shepherd at our house in South Boston."

The smiles on their faces seemed to light up as they petted Spike. Nothing like a dog to break the ice, thought Sebastian. The shorter one appeared to be a little younger. Although she wore a head cover, her color and and build implied a Scotch-Irish background. The other nun, who referred to herself as Sister Cynthia, appeared to Sebastian to be of Italian ancestry, with her darker hair and olive skin. She definitely had a strong "Southie" Boston accent. They were both very nice to Sebastian, opening up about their childhoods. After talking for close to an hour, they both said they had to go to prayer time. They hugged Spike and waved goodbye to Sebastian.

After they left, Sebastian and Spike decided to walk around the neighborhood, maybe pick up some granola and fruit. The sun was getting low in the sky and casting shadows behind them against the backdrop of a decaying city infrastructure. As they passed people walking on the street or sitting on their steps, Sebastian recognized that it was obvious that he wasn't from this area. His look, demeanor, and attitude were from a more open, confident, and curious place. He said hello to people as he walked but got few replies, just blank stares. He found a small grocery store where he picked up an apple and a pear. They didn't have any granola, although there was a small bag of dog food. Sebastian and Spike walked back to the church twenty minutes before the doors were going to be locked.

Sebastian washed up, grabbed a paperback book, snuggled up in his bed, and began to fall asleep very quickly. Spike lay on his rug beside his master. Later that night, Spike was awoken by the sound of voices. One voice was not very friendly which made Spike very aware, and he nudged Sebastian to wake up and open the door. Out in the hallway was a man in his thirties wearing a black t-shirt, gray pants, and sneakers. He was of mixed race, about 5 feet 11inches tall and about 215 pounds. He was carrying what appeared to be a gold cross and a statue of Jesus. Evidently, he had just stolen them from the chapel when the younger nun that Sebastian had met confronted him.

"Why are you here at this time of night? And what are you doing with those religious articles?"

"Shut up," he said and pushed her to the ground.

Spike had been watching from the doorway and suddenly sprang to his feet and jumped into the thief's midsection. The startled thief fell backward to the hard floor. Spike continued growling and trying to bite the man who was kicking and punching at him. By this time, the commotion had alerted others in the building who called the police and came and restrained the man until the police arrived. Most of the restraining was done by Sebastian and the building superintendent. When the police arrived, they charged the man with breaking and entering, larceny, and assault. Soon after the police left, most everybody went back to their rooms and tried to finish their night's sleep.

In the morning, the place was abuzz with talk about the happenings that had taken place in the middle of the night. Praise was being heaped upon Spike. All the nuns were hanging around the kitchen discussing the incident, and each wanted to give Spike a treat. Sebastian was quietly taking a back seat to his brown-and-white traveling buddy. Nobody had recognized the assailant; apparently, he was not a member of the parish. Father Ryan came in the room. He lived in a small house that sat adjacent to the church. He was asking questions about the night before. He wanted to know if anybody had been hurt. Although Sister Kathryn had been knocked to the floor, she had no lasting injuries. Sebastian and the building superintendent indicated that they had not been injured either.

"What about your dog?" he asked.

"Spike is fine, too."

Just then, a news reporter from WTVG came with a camera crew. The reporter introduced herself as Rose Cannaday. She'd seen the police report and thought there might be a good story behind it. She began to interview the priest, asking about the value of the items that had nearly been stolen from the church. The priest said both items had been given to the church in the 19th century by the Vatican. They were both made of gold and silver, but the statue of Jesus was the more valuable of the two. He explained that no other items had been in danger of being stolen.

The reporter began to inquire about the actual crime and wanted to speak with the subject of the assault. She asked to speak to Sister Kathryn. Sister Kathryn agreed to speak as long as no cameras or microphones were present. Ms. Cannaday asked if the intruder had tried to sexually assault her, which the sister emphatically denied. Sister Kathryn was describing the actual scenario when a light bulb went on in the reporter's head as to what a story she had. Here was a devout person of the cloth being attacked inside her place of residence, when a lovable springer spaniel, who just happened to be staying the night, comes to her rescue. Instead of a knight in shining armor, it's a dog with wagging tail.

Since cameras were off for Sister Kathryn, Spike became the focus of the story. Ms. Cannaday knew she had a blockbuster of a human interest story. She immediately called her editor and asked that more time be given for this story. She then knocked on Sebastian's door and asked if he and Spike would consider giving an interview. Sebastian agreed, and she quickly brought the cameraman into the room to film Spike. She asked Sebastian to go over the whole fight scene in detail. Of course, once that was finished, she inquired about why they were staying there in the first place. It was déjà vu again as he began to summarize their journey. The reporter kept thinking how this story kept getting better and better.

Once the story hit the twelve o'clock news, the newspapers picked it up. Reporters were crawling around the church grounds, all hoping to get pictures of Spike and Sebastian. Spike's snapshot and story were all over the Toledo papers by late afternoon. Of course, all this publicity led to invitations for interviews. Since Sebastian wasn't in a hurry to hitchhike that day, he agreed to one, to help raise money for the local SPCA. At the end of the evening, he was glad to be dropped back at the church, in the peacefulness and quiet of a Catholic communal edifice.

When he got back to the church, Sebastian welcomed the serenity of his little room and the easy conversations with the sisters. A few of them remarked how they had seen Sebastian and Spike on the evening news, and it was actually good news for the Church. In an era of moral decay and diminishing Catholic church attendees, any publicity for the Church was good.

The following morning, Sebastian awoke and went to the kitchen for some cereal and coffee. Sisters Kathryn and Cynthia were there along with a couple of others. The others were a few years older, and they asked if they could take Spike outside and throw a ball to him for retrieval. Sebastian was happy to oblige. It would give Spike some exercise and potty time, and him time to relax. He was happy to talk to the two nuns about their backgrounds and how they knew this was their calling. They both agreed that it was not always easy, making that type of life choice, but they both knew in their souls that a semi-monastic life had been good for them.

Sister Cynthia had been raised in a strong religious environment, where the men were expected to find success in the work world and the women were expected to stay home and have children. She said she had no desire for that life. Sister Kathryn said she had been rebellious from a young age and had done some things to get herself into trouble in her community. She admitted that she was partly forced to enter the sisterhood of the Catholic Church, but now she was glad she did. Both had enjoyed sports while in school. Sister Kathryn said she was pretty good at field hockey, while Sister Cynthia proved that urban life gave basketball the priority. Sebastian asked if either of them had ever had a desire for a husband and children. Both said that had never been their highest priority. In the end, they both agreed that they were content to follow their chosen path.

Sebastian was getting ready to leave but wanted to thank Father Ryan. Sadly, the priest had to leave to preside over the burial of a parishioner. It disappointed Sebastian very much to leave without personally thanking the priest for his graciousness and hospitality. Instead, he left a thank-you poem with Spike's paw print.

> At times the world is aflame
> With Evil and Distress
> But there is always Hope
> And the need to feel Safe
> We just need to look within
> And find our inner Faith
> Our Faith may have different paths
> Depending from where we came
> But ultimately, the morality and
> Virtuous Goals are pretty much
> The Same
> Lots of love
> Sincerely,
> Sebastian and Spike

The two then found their way to the interstate, and once again the journey continued.

Chapter 20

Sebastian and Spike managed to make their way to Route 75, and from there they were dropped off where Interstate 90 intersected 75. It was a sunny, warm Friday morning. It was rush hour, and Sebastian was holding Spike very close with a tight leash to avoid oncoming traffic. He was getting a little impatient when a nice Cadillac Seville pulled over and asked where they were going. Sebastian quickly said Pennsylvania.

"Great. I'm going to Pittsburgh. Is that okay with you?"

Sebastian nodded and the man popped the trunk for Sebastian's backpack. After they got in the car, the gentleman introduced himself as Murray. Sebastian reciprocated with their names. Murray was well dressed, wearing a gray pinstripe suit, blue shirt with silver cuff links, a navy blue tie with matching breast pocket handkerchief. Sebastian thought this man had a nice way about him. He was handsome, had a big smile, appeared to be in his mid-fifties, and had partly gray, curly hair.

"Have you been traveling long?" asked Murray.

"Several months, and we are just about finished."

"Has it been worth the journey?"

"Absolutely. We wouldn't change a thing. We had experiences that you can't predict or buy. Excuse me, sir, if you don't mind, can I ask you a question? How come you stopped and picked us up?"

The man replied, "I have a son about your age, and he is somewhere out in San Francisco, living a life very different from mine. I know he hitchhikes places, doesn't have many possessions, so you reminded me of my son."

Sebastian thanked him for that answer and began inquiring

about his children. Once he started talking about his children, Murray's face beamed with joy. He had three children: Marvin age 26, Sharon age 21, and Shelley age 19. He said his oldest, the heir to the family name was the one living in San Francisco. He had graduated from Duquesne University with a degree in engineering and then had gone to University of Pittsburgh for a Master's in Computer Science, but he dropped out after one year. He then traveled around to different communes before ending up in San Francisco.

"Believe it or not, he was a great athlete in high school and had a high IQ. I hope he is just going through a phase right now.

"My daughter Sharon just graduated from Penn State University with a degree in biology. She has been accepted at the University of Virginia Medical School in the fall. In fact, she is getting married tomorrow. Pretty exciting time."

"Who's the lucky guy?" said Sebastian.

"His name is Steven Bloomberg. He is from Allentown, Pennsylvania. He majored in business and is an independent sales representative. He carries several medical products. What's good is that he can live where Sharon has to be, because he can work from home a lot. Much of his work is on the phone. My other daughter, Shelley, is a student at University of Pennsylvania. She is majoring in nutrition. She wants to design better diets for healthier living."

"Sounds like you and your wife have done a great job raising your children. May I ask what you do for a living?" said Sebastian.

"Sure, I own several food franchises. I never went to college. My family was poor, so I learned to work hard at a very early age. I saved my money, and when fast food started to gain popularity, I bought a few franchises. I got into McDonald's, and they have been very prosperous. America is rapidly going through serious changes in eating habits. More households are needing two people to have gainful employment to make ends meet, and under that premise, eating out cheaply is becoming more necessary for success."

Murray and Sebastian carried on a conversation ranging from the rise of fast food to Vietnam and the counter-culture that began in the '60s and was continuing into the '70s. All the while they were talking, the Cadillac careened to Route 80, 480, and then Route 76, better known as the Pennsylvania Turnpike. Spike was resting quietly on the large back seat of the Seville.

"So, are the wedding plans all set and ready?"

Murray replied, "Absolutely. We don't leave things to chance."

Murray said that his family was of the Jewish faith and would attend their synagogue in the morning. He explained that the Sabbath of the Jewish faith began at sundown on Friday evenings and ended at sundown on Saturday. He said that the Jewish religion was mostly broken into three divisions in America. The Orthodox Jews followed the Torah and rules much more strictly than the others. They often don't work or do anything except pray on the Sabbath. Many will not even drive a vehicle. They eat kosher, which in simple terms means the food is blessed by a rabbi, and their kitchens have separate meat and dairy areas. They do not eat pork. They mostly wear black suits and white shirts, have beards, and wear what American's call skullcaps.

He then said that Conservative Jews were more Americanized and didn't follow the rituals and rules as strictly. It didn't make them less spiritual. Many still kept a kosher kitchen. They just blended into the larger society a little more. He admitted that his family belonged to this group. Both groups insisted marriage be between Jews. Marriage to a person outside the faith wasn't recognized.

"There are many more differences that would take a while to discuss. The third movement is the most liberal of the three, called Reform Judaism. They still follow the Torah but are much more progressive in their outlook. They will recognize a mixed marriage, but they encourage the gentile to convert to Judaism. They want the mother to be Jewish. There is also a small group called Reconstructionists who do not believe that the Jews are the chosen people."

"I guess people are different and will see things differently in all faiths. This is good as long as people respect other opinions," said Sebastian.

They were getting close to Pittsburgh when Sebastian said to Murray, "If you need any help in preparing for the wedding, I would be glad to help. It's the least I can do after you've shown us the hospitality of your vehicle."

"I'll have to talk to my wife, but if you really want to help, I'm sure there are a lot of last minute details to take care of."

"If you have a backyard, I could set up my tent, and Spike and I would be no problem."

"Nonsense. We have a small apartment above our garage. You can stay there."

The Cadillac came through Pittsburgh by downtown, passed the University of Pittsburgh, and drove to a neighborhood called Squirrel Hill. They pulled into the driveway of a modern house, which looked like it was built in the '60s. The house had a two-car detached garage and a fenced-in backyard. Above the garage was an apartment with two windows that had shades and curtains over them.

Murray told his wife to come out into the driveway, that there was someone he wanted her to meet. The screen door opened, and a middle-aged woman about 5 feet 6 inches tall and maybe 140 pounds came out. She had neck-length frosted hair and wore a bright-colored sundress, mostly red and orange, which hung below her knees. She had a pleasant smile as she approached.

Murray said, "This is Sebastian and his dog, Spike. I told them they could stay above the garage for the weekend. Sebastian offered his services to help out with the wedding in any way you need." He turned to Sebastian. "This is my wife, Harriet."

She looked a little shocked at first but quickly recovered and said, "If you're good enough for my husband, it's good enough for me. Welcome to our house. I must tell you, tonight is the beginning of the Sabbath, so we will go to the synagogue for a little while. We will eat early, and Sebastian, you are welcome to have dinner with us."

"Thank you very much. I assure you I will not be a burden on your busy weekend."

"Since you've asked, I will put you to work. I will make out a list, because there are many things to take care of. The schedule is we go to the synagogue tomorrow afternoon, where my daughter Sharon will be married. She is marrying a man named Steven Bloomberg. From the actual wedding, we will go to the country club for the reception. We have our older son's clothes in his closet. You look about his size, so you are welcome to pick out anything to wear tomorrow. Is that okay?"

"Absolutely. I welcome it, and I thank you for the hospitality."

Sebastian and Spike went up to the loft above the garage. It was very comfortable. In fact, it was much more comfortable than he had been used to. He showered, took Spike for a walk, and then got ready for dinner. When he entered the dining room, he was greeted with "Shalom Shabbat" and given a yarmulke to wear on the top of his head. There were ten people at the table already. Murray, Harriet, Sharon and Steven, Shelley and her boyfriend, Kenny, the groom's parents, and Sharon's grandparents. Sebastian couldn't believe that he had been invited to this special occasion. Murray got up and said a prayer called the "Kaddish," and everyone sipped some Manischewitz wine. Murray had two challah bread loaves, which looked like bread in knots. He recited a small prayer called a "HaMotzi" and then broke the loaves into pieces and handed them out to everyone at the table. After that, they began to eat wonderful, tasty food.

It was a joyful time. Sharon looked like she was on cloud nine, continually beaming her eyes toward Steven. Shelley kept staring at Sebastian when her boyfriend wasn't looking.

"What's he doing here?" she asked.

So Murray told everyone Sebastian's story to keep all the wondering in check. They served Sebastian some gefilte fish with horseradish, which he ate but was not too thrilled about. Next, he was served chicken soup. He sipped only the broth. The main meal consisted of stuffed salmon, baked chicken with kishke, potato kugel, fried eggplant, creamed broccoli, cholent, and babaganoush. Several delicious desserts followed. Sebastian didn't eat it all, but he tried at least to taste most of it.

During the meal, Sebastian tried to remain quiet so as not to take the attention from the bride- and groom-to-be. The meal lasted about an hour, and then everyone walked the two blocks to the synagogue. Sebastian went back to the loft and brought Spike some leftovers.

Sebastian and Spike stayed in the loft for the rest of the night. On Saturday morning, Sebastian took Spike for a walk and then went to see if he could help out. Harriet was grateful, for there was a lot to do. She first demanded that he have breakfast. He agreed and was brought a bagel and lox sandwich with cream cheese, onions, and tomato. Also on the plate was a piece of smoked whitefish. Sebastian had never had this before but enjoyed the flavor.

Right after breakfast, Harriet asked if Sebastian wouldn't mind mowing the lawn. Sebastian was happy to be of use in this busy time and quickly got to work. After mowing, he went about helping to straighten up the house because, after the reception, some close friends might come back to the house. During this time, Sebastian asked Murray and Harriet about their Jewish faith and heritage. They gladly answered his questions as best as they could.

Throughout the morning, Shelley kept finding ways to pass near Sebastian. She seemed to be trying not to be obvious, but Sebastian soon became aware of her actions. After all the chores were done, Harriet brought Sebastian a navy blue pin-striped suit, a blue button-down long-sleeved shirt, a red tie, and a pair of black leather shoes. She asked if they would fit. He looked at the size, and then put them on. They were a little big, but he still could wear them.

The time had come to attend the wedding. The group had two limousines waiting for them outside the house. The first was a black Cadillac for the bride and her parents and grandparents. The second was a gray Lincoln for the sister, her boyfriend, and two very close neighbors. Somehow, Sebastian was asked to join them. He felt like the missing brother's stand-in. In the limo, he sat to the left of Shelley. He noticed that she kept getting closer to him during the ride. Not one to create a situation, Sebastian looked out the window pretending not to notice. When the limo pulled up to the synagogue, Shelley put her hand on Sebastian's thigh, pushing herself up.

She turned around and said, "Oh! I'm sorry. I didn't notice where my hand was." She smiled as she stepped out of the car.

As they walked into the house of worship, Sebastian was handed a yarmulke, which sat on top of his long curly hair. He followed the group to the front and joined the family in the second row. He could see people looking at him and whispering, like who is that person with the family? The wedding ceremony began with Sharon dressed in a long, flowing, lace wedding gown. It looked as if it had been made by hand. It covered her shoulders and revealed just a little cleavage at the top. She walked down the aisle like she was walking on clouds. Shelley was the maid of honor, dressed in a pink dress with matching corsage. Her hair hung down below her neckline. She led the other four girls in the wedding party.

After all were in place, the rabbi greeted the bride and groom and began to lecture them on the responsibilities of accepting their wedding vows. He stressed the end of a singular life, that now they shared a bond which would extend to all facets of their lives. Family is supreme in the Jewish household, and the marriage vows were acceptance of a new life, under the eyes of God. After many minutes of the rabbi speaking to them in English, he spoke some words in Hebrew to the couple and the congregation. The cantor sang a song in Hebrew, and the rabbi called the couple together to exchange vows. The groom's best man handed them the ring. The rabbi then pronounced them man and wife, at which point they stepped on a glass wrapped in a white napkin and heard it shatter. The couple then turned to face the congregation, and cameras began flashing. Women had tears in their eyes. It was a joyous time for all involved.

As the bride and groom walked out of the synagogue, all the people stood and clapped. The flash of light bulbs in the cameras lit up the room. The couple walked out to the hallway, followed by their immediate families. They all stood and greeted all the friends and relatives who had attended the service.

Once the receiving line wrapped up, the group got back in their limos and went to the reception hall at a posh Pittsburgh hotel. No expense had been spared. There was an open bar that included all the premiums, a live six-piece band, and tables to seat hundreds of people. While the immediate family was posing for pictures with the photographer, Sebastian wandered around the room tasting hors d'oeuvres and taking in the scene.

A woman in her early thirties came up to him and said, "Excuse me, but I couldn't help noticing you with the family. I have known them my whole life and have never seen or heard of you. I don't mean to be rude, but who the hell are you?"

Sebastian laughed. "I'm an acquaintance of Marvin. He had some pressing engagements in San Francisco and wanted to come but couldn't, so he sent me in his place."

That quick-thinking response seemed to smooth things and satisfy her curiosity. Sebastian enjoyed some of the food, like the shrimp dishes and the bruschetta made with mini bagels. However, he stayed away from the meat dishes.

Finally, the moment came when the band began playing music as the bride and groom came in followed by their families. Sebastian was seated next to Shelley, in a seat that had been saved for Marvin, in case he had shown up. Everyone then sat down and was served a wonderful prime rib dinner with potatoes and asparagus. The appetizer was French onion soup. The few vegetarians in the group were offered either crab cakes or spaghetti. Sebastian chose the crab cakes, which were scrumptious.

After the meal, the band leader called the bride and groom to have their first dance together, followed by the father of the bride with his daughter, and then the mother of the groom with her son. Then, the rest of the relatives and friends were invited to the dance floor. As the alcohol began to flow more, the room became boisterous, and many of the guests got out on the dance floor. The band then played "Hava Nagila," and everyone joined hands and sang along. It seemed to be a very traditional song for the Jewish people.

For dessert, there was a three-layer mousse cake and, later, the wedding cake. The wedding cake was three-tiered with bride and groom figures on top. The first slice cut out revealed that it was red velvet with cream cheese inside and a white cream cheese icing on the outside.

Later in the evening, the band announced that the couple was going to leave, and everybody danced with the bride and gave her some money for the honeymoon. Of course, this was in addition to the gift that was given on arrival. The couple then left in their limo for the airport to fly to Miami Beach for their honeymoon. The party lasted awhile after they left. The older folks left shortly after the bride and groom, but the younger guests stayed and danced and drank until late. The younger teens snuck around, stealing cigarettes off the tables and smoking them outside.

Sebastian was getting anxious to get back to the house. He needed to let Spike outside for a walk and feed him. Shelley asked him if he needed a ride back to the house. She had told her boyfriend that she was getting tired and wanted to go home. Sebastian nodded. Even though he was wary about her intentions, he wanted to get home. On arrival at the house, Shelley told her boyfriend that she would call him tomorrow, that she was exhausted and wanted to get straight to bed. He was a little irked at the hurried good night, but kissed her goodnight and went home.

Sebastian had just closed the door to the loft when he heard a knock. It was Shelley.

"Do you mind if I see your dog? He's so cute, and I don't get to pet dogs very often."

Sebastian agreed but knew she had alternative motives. Shelley said that she wanted to change out of her wedding clothes and would be back. Sebastian also removed his suit and tie and gently hung them up in the closet. He quickly put on his jeans and t-shirt. As he was wiping the shoes that he had borrowed, the door swung open. There stood Shelley wearing very short cut-off jeans and a tank top with no bra. Her hair was brunette and long, with bangs over her forehead.

She was well endowed and as she bent down to pet Spike, she deliberately leaned over leaving her cleavage in full view of Sebastian's eyes. Sebastian, being fully aware now of her motives, started asking her about her relationship with her boyfriend, like how long they had been together and if they were pretty serious. Shelley, trying her best to avoid such conversation, began to evade the subject and bring the talk back to Spike.

Sebastian had an uneasy feeling about this situation. He was a guest of such nice people and didn't want to create any household discord. He continued to ask about her boyfriend, and she said it was basically a convenient situation for both of them but that she saw no long-term future there. She was leaving an opening for new relationships. She then got on the floor and began to pet Spike, leaning back so her cleavage was right below Sebastian's eyes.

She asked how he had met her dad and a little about his background. Sebastian was telling her about their journey, when she gently leaned back a little further and pressed against his knees. Then, she swung her arm around and leaned on the top of his knee as they talked. Her left hand was petting Spike's head and her right was on Sebastian's lap.

Feeling very uncomfortable, Sebastian got up and began to pack his belongings. Even though she was cute, he felt this was not a wise avenue to travel down. Each time she made a move to make physical contact, he made an opposing move to avoid it. Sebastian now understood a little of what girls go through on many of their dates. After a while, Shelley got the hint that Sebastian was not going to have an affair in his garage loft. She backed off and said she had things to do. Sebastian was relieved.

After Sebastian took Spike for a walk, he went back to the main house and began to help clean up and get ready for the family and friends who would come back to the house. Marvin and Harriet arrived first, tired but extremely happy and satisfied with the whole wedding. Harriet asked Sebastian if he wouldn't mind being the bartender, serving wine, beer, and simple cocktails. He nodded and went about gathering the necessary items at the bar. Marvin came back and asked him what he thought of the wedding. Sebastian said he was impressed with the atmosphere and the joy that all had. He then thanked Marvin for his invitation. Marvin asked what his plans were. Sebastian replied that he and Spike would be leaving early in the morning. Marvin said he would gladly take him back out to the interstate.

Sebastian was the focus of curiosity during the rest of the evening. He answered many questions. Most people wanted to know why he was hitchhiking around and not getting a job or going to school. Sebastian deflected the question, pointing to the conundrum that "one must know thyself first, before any lifelong choices should be made."

Sebastian stayed up until everyone left and helped with the final cleanup. Harriet went over and hugged him.

"Thank you for all that you have done here, but most of all thanks for your calm, soothing presence. You have made us all feel something that we might have forgotten in our hurried, busy lives."

Spike and Sebastian got up early, said goodbye, and got in Marvin's Cadillac. At the interstate ramp, Marvin waved goodbye and drove away, leaving Sebastian with a bagel and lox with cream cheese, tomato, and onion, wrapped in aluminum foil.

Chapter 21

Sebastian and Spike once again performed their ritual of standing at the entrance to the interstate, appearing as non-threatening as possible. It hadn't even been an hour before a couple in a Chevy Impala convertible, the top down, stopped and asked if they wanted a ride. The couple were in their early thirties, dressed casually but nice. He wore a white and blue golf shirt with khaki pants and cordovan penny loafers. He appeared to be about 5 feet 11 inches tall and about 170 pounds. His blonde hair hung just over his ears. He wore gold wire-rim glasses. He had a scar on his forehead near the right temple, which he tried to hide with his hair.

She had a delightful smile and long blonde hair hanging over her shoulders, with bangs parted over her forehead. She donned a bright, lime green and purple sundress with lime green and purple costume necklace and matching bracelets. Her earrings were violet stars that hung below her lobes. She appeared to be about 5 feet 6 inches tall and weighed probably in the area of 140 pounds. She was wearing an ankle bracelet which had the name Tatayana engraved on it. Her footwear was simple leather flip-flops.

The woman said, "You must be exhausted out in the sun all day. We are glad to contribute to your journey, if that's all right."

Sebastian replied, "Absolutely," and Spike wagged his tail.

They got into the back of the car. She continued talking, but the man didn't say too much. After a while, she apologized for not introducing themselves.

"My name is Anastasia, and his is Sergey. We are eventually heading to Washington, D.C., but have to make a stop in upstate Pennsylvania. Are you in any hurry to get to your destination?"

Sebastian replied, "Not particularly."

The conversation was mostly one-sided, as she could really expel a lot of words in a short period of time. The breeze in the back of the car felt good, and Spike liked it as his ears were horizontal for much of the time instead of hanging down. After a while, they decided to stop for lunch at a Pennsylvania diner that was right off the interstate. They invited Sebastian to join them. He agreed but first had to get Spike some food and water, which he quickly did and then met them in a booth in the diner.

"We are glad to see you made it to dinner. Was Spike thrilled with his dinner?" asked Anastasia.

"Just in ecstasy," Sebastian said with a smile.

They had a pleasant meal. Anastasia had a turkey and Swiss cheese with mayonnaise, lettuce, and tomato on rye bread. Sergey ordered a cheeseburger with onions, spicy mustard, and Swiss cheese on a sourdough roll. Sebastian ordered a grilled cheese sandwich with tomato. While waiting for their food, the couple questioned Sebastian about his background and goals in life. Sebastian wasn't sure, but he believed they had ulterior motives, rather than just being friendly. After answering a lot of questions, Sebastian turned the tables and seriously questioned them about their history and goals. He could tell that they weren't being completely truthful, which made him wonder what they were trying to hide. Sebastian perceived them to be decent people and didn't think they were evil. They just weren't telling the whole story.

"So tell me. What exactly do you both do for a living?"

"We work as international teachers," said Sergey.

By his inflection, Sebastian understood that he was trying to end that topic of conversation.

Back on the road, Sebastian kept questioning them. They finally decided to trust their secret with Sebastian.

Sergey turned and said to Sebastian, "I'm sorry we were so evasive, but we had to make sure you were the right stuff for our program. Anastasia and I are committed to the overthrow of the Soviet Union. It is our life goal to see the Soviet Union break apart. We believe that the uprising in Hungary in 1968, when the Soviets brutally crushed the protest, will ultimately lead intelligent people to put down such an archaic institution. We are trying to recruit people to infiltrate the Soviet Union and get average Russian people to organize and create a free society within the Soviet Union. We believe that can only happen from within. We are part of a progressive thinking group which will try anything possible to loosen the grip of the Communist Party on the freedom of the people within the Soviet borders."

Sebastian asked, "Why is this such a secret in the United States? I would think that the State Department would gladly back all such actions."

"Covertly, yes, but outwardly they don't want to increase the Cold War tension by publicly stating they are trying to overthrow the Soviet Empire."

"Why are you confiding this to me?" asked Sebastian.

"You may take this the wrong way or as a compliment, but I will tell it to you straight. First of all, you fit the model for many of our recruits. Your age, the fact that you seem not to have put down roots anywhere. Also, the fact that you seem to easily connect with people plays a part in you being a possible colleague. However, after talking with you, we realize you have the intelligence to be quite an asset to our cause. Since you asked, we wanted to give you time to think about it. We are not a profit-making company, and we cannot pay you a salary, but we can cover expenses and give you some money for your personal use. What we offer is an experience that you cannot acquire in a safe, non-confrontational existence. We will be stopping somewhere in Pennsylvania before we drop you off, and we would like you to accompany us and see a little of our vetting process. How do you feel about that?"

"I would like that," replied Sebastian.

The Chevy convertible continued on Interstate 80 as the Russian couple and Sebastian conversed. Spike just chilled on the back seat. The day wore on, and when a highway sign that said Bellafonte appeared, their car slowed down with its right turn signal clicking. They pulled off the Interstate and headed north on Route 15. After about twenty minutes, the vehicle turned on a small back road that didn't even have a state route number. Due to the heavy foliage and brush along the road, it was hard to see anything. Another half hour and the car drove up a gravel drive and came to a compound with many buildings. It was hard for Sebastian to believe that this organized, clearly well-funded compound was not funded by the U.S. government.

Sergey turned and said, "Welcome to the world's greatest defense against totalitarianism. I want you to explore the compound and look in all the buildings. You may even inquire about what is happening. I just want you to know that everything you see and hear today stays here. You may not tell the outside of what is happening here. This is just a precaution, not because we feel that we are doing something wrong, but we don't want to endanger our main goal, which is the ending of the Soviet Union."

Just then Anastasia approached and began pointing to each building and telling Sebastian what each one was for.

"The white, metal building to the right houses the language development section. There, we teach various Eastern European languages and, also, Russian language dialects. In the building to the left of that, we teach Soviet government, culture, and history. The concrete building straight ahead is used as a testing center for possible recruits. They have to take psychology classes, history classes, and culture studies of the various Soviet entities. We have meeting rooms where we discuss and eliminate anyone who doesn't fit our needs very well. The building you see at ten o'clock includes studies in weaponry. We try to prepare for any situation.

"Each person is evaluated for specific personality, attributes, and skills. For instance, someone with a tremendous voice may help with radio messages across the Iron Curtain. Someone with tremendous people skills may be inserted within a country to try and foment change. Just for example, someone with music ability may be used to write or sing songs which foster our cause. Even writing a rock-and-roll song may produce dissatisfaction with the Soviet control system. We want the youth to promote change. You see, most revolutions start with the youth and end up succumbing to the organization of an older, more influential leadership. The youth in Eastern Europe are very dissatisfied with their lot in life. We see a generation of bright young people eager for stimulation, to get away from their drab Soviet style of life.

"Why don't you and Spike roam around the compound and observe for yourselves?"

Sebastian agreed and the two disappeared behind one of the

buildings. Sebastian went inside the language center and told Spike to wait outside. Inside the building, Sebastian saw that it was separated into ten distinct rooms. All of the rooms had sound insulation so as not to disturb people in adjacent rooms. Each room was dedicated to a specific Eastern European country, focusing on culture, food, language, history, and economy and finance. The walls had maps of the region. The library had books on the nation's cooking heritage, musical history, and general culture. A good part of the room had small areas designed for language learning. There were a few people sitting with headphones while Sebastian was touring. After spending some time, Sebastian exited the building, but Spike wasn't around. Sebastian wasn't too worried. The compound wasn't a place where Spike could get lost easily. He called out to Spike, but he was a no show.

Sebastian went into the next building. It appeared to be much more technical. One room had all the equipment that a radio broadcasting station would have. It seemed that this is where they trained people to speak across the wall over the airwaves. While looking around, Sebastian noticed other machines that looked like early rectangular computer models, each standing eight feet tall and eight feet wide. He wondered what kind of information these computers were processing. This outfit must be very well funded, because they didn't seem to be skimping on the latest equipment. The next room held IBM and Xerox machines as well as printing machines. He thought this must be where they learn to publish pamphlets and forge Communist identifications and whatever was needed. Of course, he wouldn't know for sure unless he decided to spend more time around here.

After spending a good amount of time, he went outside to look for Spike. He called, but still no Spike. He continued to walk around and then saw Spike with something in his mouth. As Spike got closer, he realized it was a stick of dynamite. Freaking out, he rushed over and grabbed it out of his mouth.

"Spike, show me where you found this. Go. Show me."

Spike took off with Sebastian following. About a hundred yards into the woods was a stash of explosives behind a large oak tree. Sebastian was surprised that such dangerous items would be left out where anybody could find them and possibly have severe unintended consequences. The question was who to tell. Sebastian was concerned that maybe somebody higher up was responsible. Meanwhile, Spike had found a stick as a replacement for the TNT. It didn't quite have the same jolt but would do for the moment. After mulling over it for a few minutes, Sebastian decided to inform Sergey.

All hell broke loose when word got out. Not only could they lose their license to have explosive materials, but if the press got hold of their project, it might very well doom it. So Sergey first had the explosives locked up and then had the TNT tested for fingerprints. Everyone who was employed there had to be fingerprinted.

Anastasia was quite pleased with Spike for his discovery. She went to the food cupboard and gave him some Ritz crackers as a treat. She was his new best friend. Sebastian kept touring the facility, seemingly very interested in the process, but he wasn't ready to commit to such a venture. Sergey pulled Sebastian aside and introduced him to other representatives.

They questioned him thoroughly. He suspected that these people were really CIA operatives in disguise. Although skeptical of their motives, Sebastian did provide them with a few ideas to reach the Eastern European younger generation. One idea was to hold sporting competitions besides the Olympics. Another was to create cultural exchanges between East and West. Anything to communicate and converse was good business. Another was to create a fake Socialist group to meet and greet behind the Iron Curtain. Even starting businesses that manufactured edible treats could show the youth that creativity and risk in the West create a better society.

Spike was hanging out with Anastasia while Sebastian was busy. After more hours, their meeting ended. They gave Sebastian a card and asked him to at least think about joining. They urged him not to reveal to anybody what he had seen. Sebastian agreed and signed a non-disclosure agreement.

Sergey mentioned that it was getting late. They could stay the night there if they wanted. Sebastian knew this was a great place to camp out, so he agreed.

Morning came quickly. As the sun slowly warmed the campus, Sebastian and Spike were out early walking around, waiting for their hosts to wake up. Spike got fed his usual dry dog food with a bowl of water. After a while, Sergey and Anastasia came out of their quarters and invited Sebastian for breakfast. It wasn't much, basic cereal, banana, coffee, and O.J., but it suited Sebastian just fine. Sergey offered to drive them back to Interstate 80, so Sebastian and Spike got their things and jumped in the back seat. They pulled away, about to begin the last leg of their trek.

Chapter 22

Sergey waved goodbye, leaving Sebastian and Spike on the interstate for, hopefully, the last leg of their journey. It wasn't very long before a white Volkswagen Westfalia pop-top camper stopped. The driver was wearing a United States Army uniform. By the two bars on his uniform, Sebastian knew that he was a captain.

"Where are you heading?" asked the officer.

Sebastian replied, "We are heading home to where we live in the Pocono Mountains in Northeastern Pennsylvania."

"Come on in then. I am passing right by that area on Interstate 80."

"Thank you very much. It's been a long trip, and we are ready for a little R&R," said Sebastian.

"That's a military term for rest and relaxation. How do you know that?"

"I was drafted into the U.S. Army during the Vietnam War and served two years. I wasn't an officer. I was an enlisted man but made it to rank of E-5."

"Thank you for serving our country," replied the soldier. "My name is Tom, and yours?"

"I am Sebastian, and this is Spike. This is a nice vehicle that you have," said Sebastian.

"Thanks. This was in a salvage yard, so I picked it up cheap and rebuilt it myself. It's great for camping, hunting, or anything to avoid motel fees. So how long have you been traveling?" asked Tom.

"Several months," replied Sebastian. "Where are you going in your uniform?"

"I'm reporting for duty. I just finished medical school and am reporting to Walter Reed Hospital to begin my residency in anesthesiology. I'm really looking forward to it, but I'm also a little nervous. The Vietnam War led to many new advances in medicine, and I will be on the forefront in bringing them to the general public. They say 'Necessity is the mother of invention,' and in wartime it is very necessary to save lives."

"How long will you serve?"

"I'm not sure. I owe them six years now. Whether I want to be a career physician, I will just have to see how it goes. They are paying my school loans, which is a huge help."

"What is anesthesiology like?"

"It's getting better all the time. Although ether is still used in a few places, new inhalation gases are making headway along with new intravenous drugs. I believe that during my career, having anesthesia will be so simple that many people will have elective procedures at the drop of a hat."

"What do you mean by elective procedures?" asked Sebastian.

"Any surgery that isn't urgent and can be postponed," replied Tom.

The conversation continued about medicine and Tom's career for a while.

"If you don't mind me asking, what are you going to do with your life when you get back home?" asked Tom.

"I'm not really sure, but I am thinking of going back to school. I still have the GI bill to use and help pay college expenses."

"That sounds like a plan to me. The future is education. Without an advanced degree, a person will be left behind. Unless they are the entrepreneurial type."

"I will definitely keep that in mind," said Sebastian.

Meanwhile, Spike was relaxing on the floor of the camper. Sebastian was a little forlorn today, thinking about the end of the adventure and the decisions he would have to make about his future.

"Where is your home?" asked Sebastian.

"I'm from the Traverse City area in Michigan, but I have been living in Chicago the last eight years for undergraduate and medical school. Now I will be working in our nation's seat of power, Washington, D.C. Who knows. Maybe I will care for the President one day."

"That would be one job under careful scrutiny."

"Absolutely. In fact, it would probably be a team of physicians making the decisions."

"Did you have to go to Ft. Bragg for basic training?" asked Sebastian.

"Yes, but as physicians, we were treated a little better than your average grunt soldier."

"When I was in, which was right after the Tet Offensive in Nam, basic training was pretty tough. I remember those drill sergeants to this day. It was best not to be noticed. You didn't want to stand out. I wasn't in great physical shape when I went in but certainly was after those eight weeks. I remember if those drill sergeants heard you call your M-16 a gun, they made you march around with one hand on your rifle and the other on your penis. Then you had to shout out, 'This is a weapon and this is my gun. This is for shooting and this is for fun.'"

"My training was a lot easier than that, thank God."

The Volkswagen was cruising along Interstate 80 and approaching the Pocono Mountains. The Poconos were long noted as the honeymoon capital of the East Coast. Resorts were set up with cabins that had heart-shaped tubs and sometimes even beds. Sebastian had previously worked at many of these resorts, doing everything from bellhop to waiter to bartender. The Poconos were only about a hundred miles from New York City and Philadelphia. Many people were beginning to build summer homes and weekend getaways there. Sebastian began to feel that he was coming home when he began to see familiar landmarks. He knew Spike would be happy to get back.

"So, do you live with your family here?" asked Tom.

"No. I have some friends who have a cabin out in the woods where Spike and I can stay until we find our own place."

The Volkswagen camper approached the Pocono Mountains. Sebastian had a little smile on his face as he saw Big Boulder and Camelback ski areas. Tom asked where Sebastian would get off. He said the Tannersville exit. The cabin was only a couple miles from there.

Tom said, "I'm not in any great rush. I can drop you and Spike off at your cabin."

Sebastian replied, "That would be great, if it's not too inconvenient."

The camper exited Interstate 80, turned up Route 611 north toward Swiftwater, and then turned up a country road until Sebastian said, "There's our place up ahead."

Tom saw two old log cabins separated by a ten-foot covered walkway. Behind the cabins on the property was a waterfall. It wasn't gigantic, but it provided a nice sound for sleeping at night. The cabins were surrounded by big oak and blue spruce trees. There wasn't any planned landscaping; it was kept more mountain authentic. Sebastian asked Tom if he wanted to come in for some coffee. Tom said thanks, but he'd better get going. They shook hands, Tom petted Spike, and they waved goodbye.

Finally, the two were back home. None of Sebastian's friends were around. They must have been either at work or on vacation. Sebastian was actually happy that no one was there. It gave him time to settle in and contemplate his experiences. Spike was running around behind the cabin, looking for squirrels and rabbits to chase. He could go to the stream and drink anytime; it was dog heaven. Sebastian put on some vinyl—Crosby, Stills and Nash—grabbed a beer from the fridge, and quickly dozed off on the couch.

Nobody came back to the cabin that night, leaving Sebastian and Spike alone. Sebastian awoke at dawn, Spike's paw swatting him because nature called. Sebastian was still thinking about the journey and what he had learned and could take away from it. Did any real lasting meaning or truth come from the trip? Sebastian wondered.

A neighbor came by and said hello. Her name was Tammy, and she brought her seven-year-old son, William. Tammy was in her thirties. She had long, thick, red hair. She was wearing faded jeans and a light blue button-down long-sleeved work shirt. Sebastian came out on the porch and began talking to her. She was really curious about his adventures and asked a lot of questions about his experiences. William was sitting on the porch drawing in his notebook with crayons and listening while they spoke.

"You really hitchhiked all the way to California and back?"

Sebastian nodded petting Spike, who was sitting close to him.

"Wasn't it hard to travel with a dog?"

"Not at all. He made the trip much more interesting. I met

people and did things I'd never have done if he hadn't been with me."

They talked for more than an hour, Sebastian recounting their many adventures and spiritual discussions. William drew and colored quietly the entire time.

After a while, William stood up and handed Sebastian a folded paper.

"This is for you," he said.

Sebastian was pleasantly surprised by this and hugged and thanked William.

"We really better get home now. My other children will be coming home."

Sebastian waved goodbye.

After they left, Sebastian opened the folded paper. There was a drawing of a person with a dog at his side and a road with cars in the background. At the bottom of the page, William had written in unsteady letters, "Yor god is alwas with yuo."

Sebastian thought about what William had written. He knew the boy was dyslexic and assumed he'd meant to write "Your dog is always with you." Sebastian thought about the many ideas of God he'd learned about. They all involved unconditional love and loyalty. God was supposed to be always with you. And he was.

"He's been there all the time, right with me, traveling at my side."

Sebastian gave Spike a tight hug and then looked at him closely.

"Thank you," he said. He looked to the clear skies and repeated to himself. "Thank you."

Spike's tail wagged.

"Let's go down to the stream for a bit, Spike. Is that okay?"

Spike barked once and the two companions made their way down to the stream.

SPIKE